CUT AND THRUST

BOOKS BY STUART WOODS

FICTION

Carnal Curiosity[†]

Standup Guy[†]

Doing Hard Time[†]

Unintended Consequences[†]

Collateral Damage[†]

Severe Clear[†]

Unnatural Acts[†]

D.C. Dead[†]

Son of Stone[†]

Bel-Air Dead[†]

Strategic Moves[†]

Santa Fe Edge[§]

Lucid Intervals[†]

Kisser[†]

Hothouse Orchid[*]

Loitering with Intent[†]

Mounting Fears[‡]

Hot Mahogany[†]

Santa Fe Dead[§]

Beverly Hills Dead

Shoot Him If He Runs[†]

Fresh Disasters[†]

Short Straw[§]

Dark Harbor[†]

Iron Orchid[*]

Two-Dollar Bill[†]

The Prince of Beverly Hills

Reckless Abandon[†]

Capital Crimes[‡]

Dirty Work[†]

Blood Orchid[*]

The Short Forever[†]

Orchid Blues[*]

Cold Paradise[†]

L.A. Dead[†]

The Run[‡]

Worst Fears Realized[†]

Orchid Beach[*]

Swimming to Catalina[†]

Dead in the Water[†]

Dirt[†]

Choke

Imperfect Strangers

Heat

Dead Eyes

L.A. Times

Santa Fe Rules[§]

New York Dead[†]

Palindrome

Grass Roots[‡]

White Cargo

Deep Lie[‡]

Under the Lake

Run Before the Wind[‡]

Chiefs[‡]

TRAVEL

A Romantic's Guide to the Country Inns of Britain and Ireland (1979)

MEMOIR

Blue Water, Green Skipper

[*]A Holly Barker Novel

[†]A Stone Barrington Novel

[‡]A Will Lee Novel

[§]An Ed Eagle Novel

CUT AND THRUST

STUART WOODS

G. P. PUTNAM'S SONS / New York

PUTNAM

G. P. PUTNAM'S SONS
Publishers Since 1838
Published by the Penguin Group
Penguin Group (USA) LLC
375 Hudson Street
New York, New York 10014

USA · Canada · UK · Ireland · Australia
New Zealand · India · South Africa · China

penguin.com
A Penguin Random House Company

Library of Congress Cataloging-in-Publication Data

Woods, Stuart.
Cut and thrust / Stuart Woods.
p.   cm.
ISBN 978-0-399-16911-3
1. Political fiction. I. Title.
PS3573.O642C88   2014   2013050462
813'.54—dc23

Printed in the United States of America
1   3   5   7   9   10   8   6   4   2

BOOK DESIGN BY NICOLE LAROCHE

CUT AND THRUST

S tone Barrington was about to leave his house for Los
Angeles and the Democratic convention when the
phone rang. "Just put the bags in the car and I'll be
right down," Stone said to Fred Flicker, his factotum.

"Righto, sir," Fred replied, and started moving cases.

Stone answered the phone on the third ring. "Hello?"

"It's Ann." He had been seeing a lot of Ann Keaton. She
was deputy campaign manager for the presidential effort of
Katharine Lee.

"Hi, I'm just leaving the house to pick you up."

"Something has come up."

Stone hated those words; he didn't like changes in his
plans, especially when they involved a transcontinental flight.
"What is it?"

"Kate needs a lift."

Katharine Rule Lee, in addition to being a candidate for president, was also the first lady of the United States, running to succeed her husband, William Jefferson Lee, and she never needed a lift anywhere.

"What, to the airport? Has the Secret Service run out of black SUVs?"

"No, to Los Angeles."

"Whatever happened to Air Force One?"

"It's just fine, thank you, but the Marine helicopter sent to take her to Dulles, where she was to meet Air Force One, is down with a broken wing, or something, and it would be much more convenient for her if she could fly with us. Is there room?"

"How big a party are we talking about?"

"Her secretary and two Secret Service agents."

"No further entourage?"

"Just me, and I was going with you anyway."

"Hold the phone and I'll call Mike."

"Right."

Stone pressed the hold button, chose another line, and called the cell phone of Michael Freeman, chairman and CEO of Strategic Services.

"Mike Freeman."

"It's Stone. I have a request—feel free to say no, but you'll regret it the rest of your life."

"In that case, yes."

"You have just agreed to fly the first lady of the United States, her secretary, and two Secret Service agents to Los Angeles on your Gulfstream with us."

There was only the briefest of silences. "Yes," Mike said again. "I can do that."

"Thank you, kind sir. See you at the airport."

"I'm already at the airport."

"Am I late?"

"No, I'm meeting with a client who's passing through."

"All right, I and my party will be on time. I can't speak for the first lady."

"That's the beauty of owning an airplane—our ETD is whenever I say it is."

"See you there." Stone disengaged and pressed the hold button again. "The answer is a resounding yes."

"Oh, good," Ann said with a sigh.

"Next question, is she ready to leave for Teterboro?"

"She's sitting in a black SUV at the East Side Heliport and she doesn't have anywhere else to go. She may beat us there."

"Tell her to meet us at Jet Aviation. It's the one with the very large white airplane parked just outside the door. I'll let them know she's coming."

"Don't do that, she doesn't like any fuss. She'll just want to pee and get on the airplane."

"Tell her she can pee on the airplane, it's equipped for that, and she'll save the bother of the Secret Service throwing everybody out of the ladies' room at Jet Aviation."

"I'll pass that on," Ann said.

"I'm leaving and I'll be there in ten minutes," he said. "Let Dino and Viv know, will you?" Dino Bacchetti, Stone's old NYPD partner, now chief of detectives, and his wife, Vivian, were coming to the convention with them, and, conveniently,

3

they lived in the same Park Avenue apartment building as Ann.

"Certainly."

Stone hung up, grabbed his jacket, and followed Fred and the luggage down to the street, where the Bentley Flying Spur sat idling at the curb, Fred already at the wheel. Stone got in. "Go. We're picking up Ann Keaton and the Bacchettis on the way."

"Righto, sir." The car glided away. "By the way, sir, my New York City gun license arrived in this morning's mail."

"Congratulations."

"All I need now is a gun."

"There's a gun shop downtown that all the cops use. Joan will give you the address. Take your license with you. And bring me the bill for whatever you choose."

"Thank you, sir. And please thank Chief Bacchetti for me."

HALF AN HOUR after collecting his guests, they pulled to a halt at the Jet Aviation FBO (fixed base operator). Dino, Viv, and Ann went ahead to the airplane while the doorman and a line-man unloaded all their luggage. Stone took the doorman aside. "Have you seen a couple of"—he looked up to see three black SUVs pull into the parking lot—"those?"

"I see them, Mr. Barrington."

"One of them contains the first lady of the United States. Please take a couple of carts and whisk her straight through the terminal and onto the G650 on the ramp." He gave the man a hundred, which always brought a doorman to attention.

"Yes indeed, sir!" The man grabbed two carts and pushed them quickly toward the caravan.

Stone waited for Kate to get out of the car and make sure all her luggage was aboard the carts, then she came and kissed him on a cheek. "Stone, you're so kind to do this."

"Save your thanks for Mike Freeman, who's waiting for us aboard the airplane."

"You haven't met my secretary, Molly Cannon." She and Stone shook hands. "And these are my Secret Service detail, Tom Brennan and Christy Thomas." He shook their hands, too.

He offered Kate an arm. She took it, and they practically sprinted from the front door to the back door, without attracting too many stares, and out onto the ramp, where the big jet sat, one engine running. The linemen got the luggage stowed while the two Secret Service agents raced aboard and made sure that no members of al-Qaeda were flying with them. Shortly, they were all settled aboard and introduced, and the airplane's other engine started.

"I'm sorry it's not Air Force One," Mike said.

"Oh," Kate said, "it will do very nicely. And for purposes of this flight, we can call it Air Force One-point-Five." She took the aisle seat next to Stone and across the table from Ann. "May I join you?" she asked.

"Of course."

"There's something I want to talk to you about while we're en route."

The airplane began to taxi up the ramp toward Taxiway Lima. As they reached it, Stone saw a dozen jets lined up and waiting for the Gulfstream to take the runway while ground control cleared it for immediate takeoff. "That's something I've never seen before," Stone said, nodding toward the waiting airplanes.

"I expect the Secret Service had a word with the tower," Kate said. "They hate my waiting in line on the ground. Somebody might take a shot at us."

"Now, that's a thought that had never crossed my mind," Stone said as the Gulfstream began accelerating, pressing him back in his seat. A few seconds later they were climbing and turning to the west.

"Oh?" Kate said. "We'll be cleared direct to Burbank. No routing or delays."

Twenty minutes later they leveled at cruising altitude, and mimosas were served.

"From now on," Stone said, "I'm going to tell Air Traffic Control that you're aboard all my flights."

"Feel free," Kate replied with a big smile.

Kate Lee waited until they had finished a salad-and-omelet lunch before placing her hand on Stone's arm. "Now," she said, "to business—or rather, to politics."

"Tell me all."

"I know from Will's experience at conventions that after our arrival and throughout our stay there will be people who will wish to talk with me who I will wish not to talk with—not because I don't like or respect them, but because their messages will sometimes be so important that they are better conveyed through intermediaries. Sometimes my messages to them will fall into the same category. Do you understand?"

"Of course. It's one of the principal reasons why people have attorneys."

"Exactly. On these occasions I will not want a campaign or staff member to act as intermediary. That would add a political edge to conversations that might be better conducted in a more civilian manner. That's why I would like you to represent me on these occasions."

"I would be very pleased to help in any way I can," Stone replied.

"Sometimes you may receive messages, at other times you may send them—sometimes both."

"I understand."

"I will always try to alert you when a call will be coming, but I won't always be able to. If someone calls you, that means he very likely got your number from me, so don't blow him off—at least, not immediately."

Stone nodded. "So if someone calls me and asks if you would accept the vice presidential nomination . . ."

"Let's hope it will be me offering it to someone else. But I hear there are other things brewing that may not surface for a few days, so be on the qui vive."

"I haven't heard that expression for decades."

"Now you're making me feel old."

"Never."

"You haven't met my chief of staff, Alicia Carey, have you? She works out of my Washington office."

"I believe I may have shaken her hand on a visit to the White House."

"Of course you would have. I hope you will have an opportunity to get to know her this week. When Alicia speaks, she speaks for me."

"I'll keep that in mind. I hope you and Will can come to dinner at my house—maybe tomorrow evening?"

"We'd both like that, but let me clear it with him."

"And, by all means, bring Alicia and whoever she'd like to bring. We'll do a buffet by the pool."

"That sounds lovely. Oh, my ears just popped, we must be descending into Van Nuys."

Molly came over. "I've just had a message—the president has landed at Van Nuys and will wait for you there. We're twelve minutes out."

"Thank you, Molly, that's good. One caravan is enough."

Stone noticed that the airplane never turned until it lined up on Runway 34 left. This was the way to travel. They touched down with a nearly imperceptible squeak of tires on pavement, and as they exited the runway, Stone saw the big 747, Air Force One, parked on the ramp, surrounded by people with weapons.

The Gulfstream came to a stop, the engines died, and the airstair door was opened. Kate was the first out of the airplane and into the arms of her husband.

"Hi, Stone," the president said, offering his hand. "Thanks for giving a girl a lift."

Stone shook his hand. "Hello, Mr. President. Thank Mike Freeman."

"It was a wonderful flight," Kate said to her husband. "Mike's food is better than ours."

A line of cars pulled up to the airplane and someone held open the door of the presidential limousine. The Lees got in. Ann kissed Stone goodbye. "See you later."

"We've got your luggage," he said.

She and Molly got into the car, following the president, and the procession moved away. Two Bentley Mulsannes from The Arrington moved into place and linemen loaded their luggage. Shortly, they were on their way.

Stone and Mike took one car, the Bacchettis the other.

"Thank you again for taking Kate," Stone said to Mike.

"It was a pleasure having her on board."

"I've asked them to dinner tomorrow night. And of course Ann and I would like you there, too."

"Mind if I bring a date?"

"Why would I mind?"

"I was thinking of asking Charlene Joiner." She was a big-time movie star who, many years before, had had a brief fling with Will Lee when he was a Senate staffer and still single.

"Ah, Mike," Stone said, "Charlene's presence near Will seems to put things a bit on edge. Do you know someone else?"

"I'll see what I can do."

"Thanks for understanding. Charlene always seems to have an ax to grind when she sees Will. For the longest time she was trying to get him to commute the sentence of her old boyfriend who was on death row for rape and murder."

"And did she get it?"

"Yes, but not from Will. When he declined, she moved down a couple of rungs and got herself fixed up with the governor of Georgia, who was happy, after a night with her, to commute the sentence to life."

"That sounds like Charlene," Mike said.

They drove on toward The Arrington.

S ecurity was already tighter than usual at the gate to The Arrington, and Stone, even though he was a major stockholder and board member, was not spared. The search of the cars was thorough.

The hotel was built on land that had been owned by Arrington's first husband, the movie star Vance Calder, and his house had been incorporated into the guest-arrival center. As part of the lease of the land to the hotel corporation, Stone had negotiated the building of a new house for Arrington. Completed after her death, he had used it as his L.A. base since the hotel opened.

His car was met by the now elderly Manolo, who had been Vance Calder's butler, and he oversaw the unloading and routing of luggage to the various rooms.

"Drinks in half an hour," Stone said to everybody, and they went to freshen up.

When he had the opportunity, Manolo approached Stone. "A man from the Secret Service was here half an hour ago," the Filipino said.

"Details?" Stone asked.

"He said he would return to brief you after the arrival of the president," Manolo said.

Brief him? About what? Stone went upstairs to his bedroom and got into some casual clothes, then he went back downstairs. A man in a suit with a lapel button was waiting to see him.

"Mr. Barrington, I'm Special Agent Mervin Beam of the Secret Service. I'm in charge of the L.A. office." They shook hands. "May I speak with you in private?"

Stone took the man into his study and they sat down. He didn't bother offering the man a drink since he knew it would be declined. "What's going on?" he asked.

"It arrived as an e-mail sent to me personally." Beam took a sheet of paper from an inside pocket and handed it to Stone. "This is a copy."

Stone read the message: *At some time before the end of the Democratic convention, Katharine Rule Lee will die. We are patriots who have sworn to return the United States to a strict, constitutional republic, and we regard Mrs. Lee as a clear and present danger to her country, since she will slavishly support the criminal policies put into effect by William Jefferson Lee.*

We have supporters in both houses of Congress and in the

government bureaucracy, and even in the Secret Service, and we have the means and expertise to carry out our promises. We are quite willing to die in pursuit of our ideals, if that should become necessary.

There will be nothing you can do to stop us. It was signed, *The Patriots.*

"WHAT DO YOU make of this?" Stone asked.

"I'm no psychologist," Beam said, "but I've seen a lot of this stuff over the years. The writer is probably an individual and there is probably no group involved. He exaggerates or, more likely, simply lies about his support in the Congress and the government."

"What about his claim of someone in your service?"

"I believe that is in the realm of preposterous."

"And his claim of the means to kill Mrs. Lee?"

"Anybody with a gun has the means to kill anybody else."

"Do you believe this man is a serious threat or just crazy?"

"Conceivably both, but in any case we will take his threat seriously, as we do all threats. The part about being willing to die is probably true—in fact, that may be what he intends."

"How did he get your e-mail address?"

Beam looked at his shoes for a moment. "That is the single most disturbing thing about the threat. I've got a tech team working on where his e-mail came from, and I've got two agents working on how he could have discovered my secure address."

"How many people have that address?"

"Knowledge of it is restricted to our director, two deputy directors in Washington, and in L.A. to three supervisory agents. It's used for the most confidential communications."

"How about secretaries, clerical workers, cleaning ladies?"

"None of the above, but an employee might root it out if he had access and enough time."

"What are your chances of backtracking to find the sender?"

"Fair to good, unless he's very, very smart and capable. We'll assume he is."

"Is there anything you'd like me to do?"

"Mrs. Lee tells me she and the president are having dinner in this house tomorrow night. I just want you to know that, from eight A.M. tomorrow, my agents will be all over the house and the property. We'll be as unobtrusive as possible."

"Actually, we'll be having dinner outdoors, by the pool, weather permitting."

"Then we'll set up a perimeter." Beam extended a hand. "May I have the e-mail back, please?"

Stone handed it to him.

"Who will be attending the dinner tomorrow night, besides the president and first lady?"

"Whoever they would like to include, plus my guests. They are Chief of Detectives, NYPD, Dino Bacchetti and his wife, Vivian, who is an executive at Strategic Services, Michael Freeman, chairman and CEO of Strategic Services, and he may be bringing someone, you can ask him. Also my son, Peter Barrington, his girlfriend, Hattie Patrick, Ben Bacchetti, the chief's son, and his girlfriend, Tessa Tweed. I'll let you know if any other guests are added to the list."

"Thank you, Mr. Barrington." Beam stood up. "I'll keep you posted if there are further developments."

"I would appreciate that." Stone shook the man's hand, received his business card, and watched him leave. Stone was not unduly alarmed about the threat, but its presence would add an edge to their evening that he didn't like. He would tell Dino and Mike to come armed.

The phone rang; Manolo answered and buzzed Stone. "Mr. Peter is on the phone," he said.

Stone picked up. "Good afternoon, kiddo!"

"Glad to hear your voice, Dad. I got your message about dinner tomorrow, and we'd all like to come."

"Great!"

"I'd also like to bring Billy and Betsy Burnett."

"Of course, I'd love to see them."

"What time?"

"Six-thirty, seven?"

"And, Dad, the night after that, we'd like to have you all over here for dinner. You haven't seen our place yet."

"I'll look forward to it," Stone said. "How's the flying going?" He had given Peter his old Citation Mustang.

"Very well. Billy has got Ben, Hattie, and me type-rated in it. Tessa hasn't shown any interest."

"Good news. You'll get lots of use out of it."

"When does your new Citation M2 arrive?"

"In a few weeks. There was a delay in certifying the avionics."

"I can't wait to see it."

"I can't wait to see you," Stone said. They said goodbye

and hung up. Stone called Mervin Beam and got his voice mail; he added the Burnetts to the guest list.

As they were having a drink before dinner, Ann turned up. "I finally got free," she said.

"Your things are in your dressing room," Stone said. "Top of the stairs, first door on your left."

"I'll go up after dinner," she said. "Right now I'd like a martini."

Stone buzzed Manolo and ordered the drink, and it appeared quickly.

"Now that I've got you all together," Stone said, "I want to tell you about my conversation with the Secret Service." And he did so.

S tone woke the following morning to find Ann in her dressing room, putting her things away. He liked it that she did these things naked.

"Good morning," he said from the doorway.

She smiled. "And good morning to you."

"If you'd like anything pressed, just leave it out and tell Manolo."

"I'll do that. Oh, by the way, Kate told me to tell you that they accept your invitation to dinner tonight with pleasure."

"The Secret Service already told me."

"Who else will be here?"

"My and Dino's sons and their girlfriends, and a couple who work for Peter in his production company at Centurion Studios, named Billy and Betsy Burnett."

"Oh, I'm supposed to tell you that Senator Sam Meriwether and his wife, Dorothy, will be coming, too."

"I've met him," Stone said, "but not her." Sam Meriwether, a former congressman from Georgia, had been elected to Will Lee's old seat and was Kate's campaign manager. His sobriquet in the Senate was "the new Sam Nunn." "They're welcome."

"Technically, he's my boss, but he's been working out of D.C., so I haven't seen a lot of him, just a lot of phone calls."

"Is he the right guy to run Kate's campaign?"

"He is. Kate wanted a southerner, preferably a Georgian, and he's the sort of senator who gets along with people on both sides of the aisle. Kate and I pretty much run the day-to-day operations, and Sam is more of a strategist. He also is good on television and gets along very well with the press."

"The accent helps, I think," Stone said.

"It certainly does. It's an old-fashioned Georgia accent, and it sounds good on him."

"Does Kate know about the death threat?"

"Sure, and she's unfazed. She's used to that sort of thing, and she knows she's well protected."

"I'm glad to hear that. I wouldn't want her to worry unnecessarily. What time do you have to be back with Kate?"

"Not until eight-thirty or so," she said.

"Then you have time to come back to bed for a little while, don't you?"

She smiled. "I'll be right there."

THEY HAD BREAKFAST sent up on trays and ate in bed, watching the morning shows and reading the papers. A BREAKING NEWS title came on the screen.

"We've just had news that Senator Eleanor Stockman has taken a turn for the worse," an anchorwoman said.

Ann put down the papers and listened. "Uh-oh," she said.

"Senator Stockman went into the hospital after collapsing at her home last week, and was diagnosed with an operable brain tumor. She had the surgery and was said to be recovering well, but in the early hours of this morning she arrested and had to be revived and intubated. She has been on a respirator for several hours now, and a spokesman says that she is in critical condition."

"That's so sad," Ann said. "I saw her in New York a couple of weeks ago, and she looked tired, but healthy. She was scheduled to speak at the convention."

"It sounds very serious," Stone said. "Who will they get to replace her?"

"My guess is Governor Richard Collins might appoint himself to the seat. He's one of our bright younger stars, and it would be a good opportunity for him to become better known nationally."

"He was the mayor of San Francisco, wasn't he?"

"That's right."

"Would he make a good vice presidential running mate for Kate?"

"Too soon. He's only thirty-eight, and he hasn't finished his first term. Pedro 'Pete' Otero of New Mexico has had two terms as governor, and—don't tell anybody this—he's the favorite for VP in our camp, if he doesn't beat us for the nomination!" She looked at her watch. "I've got to get into a shower and run over to the presidential cottage," she said, getting up and trotting toward her bathroom.

Stone finished the papers and was just getting up when she left. He showered, shaved, and dressed and got downstairs in time to see Mike Freeman and Dino about to leave.

"We're off to a security meeting with the convention managers," Mike said. "Chief Rivera of the LAPD has asked Dino to come along and kibitz."

"Good for you to get to know your future peers around the country," Stone said.

"Don't start," Dino said.

"We'll be back in time for a drink before dinner," Mike said. "Oh, I didn't make another date for dinner."

"How did Charlene take your breaking your date?"

"Like an arrow in the chest, I think."

"I wouldn't be surprised if she just showed up," Stone said.

"You really think she'd do that?"

"She won't if I alert the Secret Service."

"Do that, and I'll never get laid again," Mike said.

"Don't worry, Charlene will have you back in the sack in no time," Stone said.

*T*he kids arrived a little early for the dinner party, and they sat out by the pool, waiting for the other guests.

"Tell me about these houses you've bought," Stone said to Peter. "You've been pretty quiet about it."

"Ben and I bought two adjacent properties in Brentwood," Peter said. "We've taken down the fencing between them and combined the landscaping, so that it seems like one larger property with two houses. We have nearly four acres, altogether. Hattie and Tessa have done the decorating, and we're ready for what amounts to a double housewarming tomorrow evening."

"I can't wait to see the place," Stone said.

"Neither can I," Dino said. "Are you sure you can afford this, Ben?"

"Dad, I'm a successful movie producer," Ben replied. "You'd be surprised at what I can afford."

Billy and Betsy Burnett arrived, Billy introduced Betsy to the grown-ups. It suddenly occurred to Stone that having the former Teddy Fay at a dinner with the first lady and the president who had secretly pardoned him could make for some discomfort. He was about to take Billy aside and talk with him about it when the presidential party arrived.

Introductions were made, and Stone watched Kate carefully. Will Lee had never seen Teddy Fay, but Kate would have when she was at the CIA. The moment passed without incident, and Stone breathed a little easier.

Stone found himself sitting between Senator Sam Meriwether and Kate Lee.

"You heard about Senator Eleanor Stockman's illness?" Kate asked.

"Yes, this morning on TV."

"I spoke with her son a few minutes ago. Eleanor is showing no sign of brain activity, and the family are discussing now whether—or rather when—to take her off the respirator."

"That's very sad," Stone said. "I had to face something like that with my mother. She died before we could bring ourselves to turn off the machine."

Kate nodded. "So many families have to face that."

Sam Meriwether spoke up. "This means we're going to have to face another event," he said. "When Eleanor dies, her Senate seat comes available, and Governor Dick Collins will appoint someone to replace her. She was reelected two years ago, so there's a four-year term before the appointee would have to face reelection."

"You see where this is going, Stone?" Kate asked.

Stone took a sip of his drink. "Might Martin Stanton be a candidate to fill her seat?"

"That's astute of you," she said. "We have to make some suppositions here, and without as much information as we'd like before doing so."

"You think Stanton would accept if it's offered?" Stone asked.

"No, I don't—at least, not before the convention."

"What if his support begins to crumble in the California delegation?"

"That would certainly point him in the right direction, but we don't see that happening, at this point."

"The thing is," Meriwether said, "if Marty knows there's a safe Senate seat waiting for him if he isn't nominated, he may not fight quite so hard to get the nomination."

"Is there someone you'd like me to speak to?" Stone asked, cognizant of his conversation with Kate on the flight out.

"Do you know Dick Collins?" Kate asked.

"I met him at a cocktail party in San Francisco five or six years ago when he was still mayor. I don't know if he'll remember, but we had a nice conversation for a few minutes."

"He'll remember," Kate said. "He has a phenomenal memory for names and faces."

Peter was sitting nearby. "Excuse me, Dad, but did I hear you mention Governor Collins?"

"Yes, you did."

"Ben and I gave him a tour of Centurion Studios a couple of days ago. We invited him to the housewarming. He said he'd get back to us. He hasn't yet."

"You have a better network than you know, Stone," Kate said. "Peter, don't ask him again. Don't worry, he'll get back to you, he never forgets anything. If he shows up, Stone, then there's an opportunity."

"Does he know that you and I are acquainted?" Stone asked.

"Stone, after that stupid rumor the opposition started about you and me, the *nation* knows we're acquainted. And Dick knows we're staying next door to you at The Arrington."

"Peter," Stone said, "when the governor calls back, tell him I'm looking forward to seeing him again at your housewarming."

"Sure, Dad." Peter went to get another tonic water, his usual drink.

"If he doesn't make the party," Kate said, "we'll find another reason for you and the governor to rub elbows."

"He'll be here for our gala," Stone said. The Arrington was hosting a big fund-raiser, where the singer and actress Immi Gotham would be performing in the hotel's amphitheater for an invited audience of 1,500 of the top party contributors.

"I think Peter's housewarming would be better—more intimate," Kate said. "Too much backslapping going on at the gala, too much flesh to press."

24

"We'll leave the gala for a backup, then," Stone said. "I'll see that we sit in the same box—that will cut the crowd down enough for us to have a word."

"These things have a way of working out," Kate said, "if we work hard enough to make them happen."

*T*hey were seated at half a dozen tables by the pool, having served themselves from the buffet, when Stone looked up and saw two Secret Service agents where they had not been before. Then there was another pair, and another. Kate affected not to notice, but Will Lee crooked a finger at Mervin Beam, and he approached the table. They exchanged whispers, then Beam walked around the area with another agent.

"Everything all right?" Stone asked the president, who was sitting across the table from him.

"I think so," Will replied quietly. "If there are any further concerns, they'll move us inside." He quickly changed the subject. "By the way, Stone, you recall the drone strike we watched together at the Carlyle a few weeks ago?"

"How could I forget that?"

26

"We've confirmed since that our effort was successful with all six of the subjects."

"Congratulations. I hope you don't have to take any heat for that."

"You know, during World War Two, we and the British killed tens of thousands of civilians during bombing raids on strategic targets in Europe—and a hundred thousand in Tokyo in a single night—and though people thought civilian raids were regrettable, they understood the reason for them. Now, when a terrorist's wife or child become collateral damage, there's an uproar."

"When an active terrorist hides in the bosom of his family, he's responsible for putting them at risk, isn't he?" Stone asked.

"My view exactly," Will said. "Unstopped, those men would have been responsible for hundreds of deaths in Middle Eastern and European cities, and perhaps some in this country. While I'm still in office, I'll keep hunting them down."

AS THE TABLE was being cleared, Beam approached the president again and whispered. Will spoke up. "You know, it's beginning to be a little chilly in this desert air, why don't we have dessert in the house?"

Stone herded the group inside, and they settled around the big living room while waiters served them dessert. Will came and sat next to Stone.

"You know, I took that e-mail to Beam more seriously than

Kate did. I'm not sure what it was, but something in that message raised the hair on the back of my neck."

"I'll certainly trust your instincts, Will," Stone said. "Nothing wrong with being cautious."

"Kate can be a little too cavalier about these things," the president said.

The party broke up around ten, and the Lees' group walked back to the presidential cottage.

"We've got to go, too, Dad," Peter said when they had gone. "This is an early town, you know."

"I've heard that," Stone said.

Peter handed him a card. "This is the address. It's a couple of blocks off Sunset. Come at six."

"I'll look forward to it," Stone said.

The kids said their good nights and left, then Stone ordered after-dinner drinks for his guests. Billy and Betsy Burnett stayed on for a drink.

"What was that about?" Dino asked. "The thing with the Secret Service?"

"They got a death threat on Kate e-mailed to them last night," Stone said. "I expect it was something to do with that, but at least nobody had to draw a weapon."

"What we need," Dino said, "is a secret method for instantly determining the location that any e-mail is sent from."

"It's being worked on," Mike Freeman said, "but don't expect to read about it in the papers. The political climate isn't good right now for new intelligence initiatives."

"I'm happy for them to read my e-mails and track my phone

calls," Stone said. "We live in a new and dangerous world, and it's not going to stop anytime soon."

"I wish I could disagree with you," Mike said.

"How did your security meeting go today?" Stone asked.

"The Democrats are going to have the most secure convention in history," Mike replied. "And Staples Center is going to be the most wired and camera-ready venue ever. Not to mention the shoe leather on the ground."

"Sounds good to me," Stone said.

"We're going to have a new shield system in operation," Mike said. "We press a button and a two-inch-thick bulletproof glass wall will rise from the floor to a height of ten feet and protects about the central third of the stage. If you see that coming up, you'll know there's a very real threat."

"Do the candidates know about that?" Stone asked.

"The Secret Service is certainly in on it—whether they'll share it with the candidates is up to them, but it will certainly go up when the nominee and the president speak."

"Very good."

"Where are your convention seats?" Mike asked Stone.

"I've got a skybox," Stone replied. "Remember? You helped me get it."

"So you have," Mike said. "From there, it will be like watching the world's largest flat-screen TV."

"And we can turn down the noise during the demonstrations on the floor. That's the part of conventions that has always bored me rigid."

"And the glass window in your box will be the same as for the platform shield," Mike said.

"That's very comforting," Stone replied. "You'll have to join us."

"I'll be in our control center," Mike said, "or patrolling the floor with a handheld radio."

"We'll wave," Stone said.

LATER, AS BILLY and Betsy were leaving, Billy called Stone aside. "I have some thoughts about that e-mail sent to the Secret Service office," he said.

"Tell me."

"It's an inside job."

"Why do you think so?"

"No one on the outside would even know of the existence of that e-mail address, but if there are half a dozen insiders who know about it, then there's a very good chance others in the office know about it, too."

"You have a very good point, Billy."

"I'd be willing to bet that if they can trace the e-mail back to one computer, it will turn out to be one in their offices."

"Then I hope they trace it back soon," Stone said, "because they're very short of time."

S tone woke early, before Ann, who slept on. When he came out of the shower she was up and dressing.

"I've got one hell of a day today," she said. "Kate has nine appointments, and I have to be with her at every one."

"Peter and Ben are having a housewarming tonight—I hope you'll be able to go. It starts early, six o'clock." He wrote down the address for her. "It's a left turn off Sunset, the other side of I-405."

"If we can keep to our schedule, Kate will be finished at four-thirty, but don't count on it. I'll call you when I'm on my way."

"Sounds good. Listen, is Kate really not concerned about the death threat?"

"Every time something like that happens, she brushes it off," Ann said, "but in her heart of hearts, who knows?"

"Not even her husband, apparently. He says she's cavalier about threats."

Ann laughed. "That's a good description. I'm going to let the Secret Service worry about it."

"Right, let them get between Kate and a bullet."

"I'm like Kate, I don't want to think about it."

"I'll see you tonight sometime," Stone said, and she was gone.

STONE WAS HAVING lunch by the pool when Peter called. "The governor has accepted our invitation," he said, "but he'll probably have to leave early. He has a lot on his plate, what with all the Democrats in town."

"I won't take much of his time."

"I'll try to see that you get a few minutes alone."

"Thanks, Peter. I'll see you tonight."

STONE LEFT THE Arrington in one of their Porsche Cayenne SUVs with a driver, instead of in a Bentley, and they drove out Sunset Boulevard to Amalfi Drive and turned left. Stone told the driver to be back at eight o'clock, then he rang the buzzer at the front gate and was let in.

He walked into some of the most beautiful gardens he had

ever seen. It always astonished Stone how things would grow in the desert soil as long as there was enough water, and clearly, there was enough water for this.

He walked up a path to a good-sized shingled house, and he could see another one very much like it next door. That would be Ben's, he reckoned. He was met at the door by Billy Burnett, who seemed to be exercising his security role.

"Good evening, Stone," Billy said, shaking his hand.

"How are you, Billy?"

"Very well, thank you. I didn't get a chance last night to thank you personally for your role in getting me the pardon," Billy said. "It's already made a big difference in my life. For the first time in many years, I can own a house."

"Where did you buy?"

"One street over from here. My property is much smaller, of course, but it backs up on Peter's property, and he's installed a gate for easy access."

"I feel better knowing you're nearby," Stone said. "For future reference, I've been warned that the Russians in Paris have not forgotten about me. Yuri Majorov had a brother, Yevgeny, who seems to have taken over his position in that organization."

"I'm sorry to hear that."

"There's been no specific threat, just a heads-up from Lance Cabot. I'll certainly be in touch if I hear anything else."

"Thank you. A part of me is accustomed to always being on guard," Billy said. A waiter appeared with a glass of Knob Creek.

Peter walked in with Hattie and greeted him just as the

doorbell rang again. Billy went to answer it and came back with the governor of California, Richard Collins. A plain-clothes officer hovered on the edge of the room.

Collins greeted everyone warmly, and a waiter brought him a drink on a silver tray. "I'm nearly the first here," he said to Stone. "Good to see you again. It's been a long time since San Francisco. My condolences on the death of your wife."

"Thank you, Governor. Would you like to sit down for a minute before the others arrive?"

"Use my study," Peter said, then led the way to a smaller room lined with bookcases. The two men took chairs in front of a fireplace, where a small blaze had been kindled.

"From everything I'm reading," Stone said, "your first term is going extremely well."

"Amazing the things you can get done when you have a majority in both houses," Collins said. "And Jerry Brown had the goodness to clean up the budget problem before I got in."

"I wanted to get your views on how the nominating process is going," Stone said.

"It's fascinating, isn't it, what Kate Lee is doing? I had my doubts at first, but I'm beginning to think she just might pull it off."

"Well, Martin Stanton has been a big help."

Collins laughed heartily. "Yes, Marty can be his own worst enemy. He's my friend, though, and I owe him my support for as long as he's in the race."

"Of course you do, and I know that Kate understands that. She'll feel differently on a second ballot, though."

"If there's a second ballot, then we're in a whole new ball game," Collins said. "And believe me, Marty knows that. It's a shame that someone with so much talent for politics and governing can risk it all for a roll in the hay. He was a terrific state legislator and governor."

"And a very good vice president," Stone said. "It has occurred to some folks that those talents might serve him well in the United States Senate."

Collins's eyes narrowed, and he smiled. "Oh, I think Marty would be good in any office in the land."

"Especially one with four years left in the term," Stone pointed out. "And I'm sure it would ease his mind to know that a soft landing is available, should the balloting at the convention not go his way."

"I'm going to take my time making that appointment," Collins said, "even though there are all sorts of people already scratching at my office door."

"I think you should certainly take your time . . . making that announcement," Stone said. "After all, timing is everything."

"Did you know, Stone, that Eleanor Stockman was taken off her respirator this afternoon about three o'clock?"

"No, I hadn't heard that. I haven't had the TV on today."

"And she died about an hour ago," Collins said. "The announcement is being made about now." He looked at his watch. "Just in time for the six o'clock news." The vibrating of a cell phone could be heard on the governor's person. He took out an iPhone and looked at it. "The deluge has already begun," he said. "I'm glad it's not Kate on the phone." He held down two buttons at once and switched it off.

"I don't expect you'll hear from her on the subject," Stone said.

"But it certainly makes our conversation pertinent, doesn't it?"

"I suppose it does," Stone said.

"Can you guess who that was on the phone?" the governor asked.

"It would be impertinent of me to try," Stone replied.

The governor laughed and polished off his drink. "Well, I suppose I'd better get in there and say hello to some folks." He stood up. "I'm told that Charlene Joiner will be here tonight," he said. "I believe you're acquainted with her, aren't you, Stone?"

"Who isn't?" Stone asked.

The governor laughed again. "She's quite a lady," he said. "Marvelous actress."

"Do you think I should get to know her better?"

"I think it would be wise to take Will Lee as your example on the subject of Charlene."

The governor smiled broadly. "Someone who was allegedly present a few years ago at Van Nuys Airport, when she tried to get to him on Air Force One, swears he heard the president tell the Secret Service that if she came on board to shoot her."

They both had a good laugh, then joined the others.

S tone walked into the living room, which was now well populated with guests, and the first person he saw was the vice president of the United States. Martin Stanton was a tall, athletically built man of about fifty, with dark hair going gray, wearing a perfectly tailored suit. He was engaged in conversation with Peter and Hattie, and his eyes flicked toward Stone as he entered the room.

Stone walked over to where they stood. "Oh, Dad," Peter said, "have you met the vice president? The governor invited him to join us this evening."

"I have not," Stone said, extending a hand, "but I am very happy to."

"I've heard so much about you, Stone," Stanton said. "I believe you and Kate Lee are very good friends."

"We are *just* good friends," Stone replied, "in spite of what you may have heard." Or spread around, Stone thought.

Stanton smiled broadly, revealing impossibly white teeth. "Of course," he said with a little smirk.

"Will you excuse me for just a moment?" Stone asked. He had seen Charlene Joiner enter the house, and he wanted to be the first to greet her.

Her face lit up as she spotted him. Charlene was beautifully attired in a silk dress and very high heels, with just the right accents of jewelry. "Stone! How are you, sweetheart?"

"I'm extremely well," Stone replied, "as you obviously are. Have you met my son and his girl?"

"I have," she replied. "We've been discussing an interesting role in his next film."

"And have you met the vice president?"

"No, but I'd like to."

"Right this way," Stone said, taking her elbow and propelling her across the room to where Stanton still stood with Peter and Hattie. "Vice President Stanton," Stone said, "may I present my favorite actress, Ms. Charlene Joiner?"

Stone watched as something clicked on in Stanton's eyes and his hand reached for Charlene's. This was the lady-killer in action, and he was about to meet his match.

"If you'll excuse us," Peter said, "we have some guests to greet."

"I'll help," Stone said, and moved away from the man and woman who were so obviously enchanted with each other. He followed Peter and Hattie toward the front door and saw Ann come in.

"Hello, there." He kissed her.

"Oh, hello," she replied. "I was nearby when Kate finished with her appointments, so I didn't bother to call."

"You didn't need to," Stone said, signaling a waiter and ordering them drinks.

"My God!" she said. "There's Martin Stanton. I want to go and say hello."

"No," Stone said, taking her arm. "Not now. He is entirely engaged at the moment, and we don't want to interrupt."

She looked at him through narrowed eyes. "You are wicked."

"They're getting along so well, why interrupt them? Why don't we go next door and see Ben's house?" He led her out a door to a terrace and found a flagstone path to the house next door. Others were streaming down it as well. As they approached the house Stone saw Ben and Tessa chatting with Leo Goldman Jr., the CEO of Centurion Studios.

"Stone!" Leo shouted, then grabbed his hand.

"Good to see you, Leo. May I present Ann Keaton?"

"How do you do, Ms. Keaton?"

"Ann is deputy manager for Kate Lee's campaign."

"I know your name well from our donor lists, Mr. Goldman," Ann said. "In fact, you're on my list to call."

Leo began slapping his pockets. "I seem to have forgotten my checkbook," he said.

"That's all right," Ann said, "I'll hunt you down later."

"Seriously," Leo said, "the check is literally in the mail."

"I'll alert the postal services."

Stone and Ann progressed into Ben's beautifully furnished house and found a pair of comfortable chairs.

"I didn't see the governor," Ann said. "He didn't make it?"

"He did, inviting the vice president, too, and he has already moved on to his next engagement."

"Then you didn't get a chance to talk with him?"

"We had a very nice chat, and we understood each other perfectly. You heard that Senator Stockman died?"

"I had a call ten minutes ago."

"Funniest thing happened as we were discussing how Stanton's gifts would so well qualify him for a Senate seat. Seconds after the announcement on the six o'clock news, the governor's phone rang, and guess who it was?"

"I've no doubt it was Marty."

"Collins didn't take the call—in fact, he turned off his phone."

"Do you think he got your message?"

"Certainly he did. He's a very astute young man, and without actually saying so, he let me know that if Stanton fails to get a majority of the delegates on the first ballot, he would be with Kate. I suggested that if Stanton knew he had the Senate seat for a backup, he might be easier to deal with at the convention."

"And how did he react to that?"

"We were in perfect agreement. Of course, he didn't say a word that would prevent him from giving the seat to someone else, or that he would support Kate if Stanton failed, but he intimated it, in the way that politicians do."

"And how did Marty and Charlene Joiner happen to meet?"

"I will cheerfully take the blame for that one," Stone replied.

"I think they're made for each other, now that Marty is functionally single again."

"I said you were wicked, didn't I?"

"You did, and I'm grateful for the compliment."

"I hope Marty can't contain himself and starts squiring Ms. Joiner around the city while everybody who is anybody in the party is in town."

"It's just the sort of brazen behavior that might help, isn't it?"

"I long to see their photograph together on every front page."

"Then we'll have to take one, won't we?" Stone said. "Or better, get Peter to." He took out his phone and pressed a speed-dial button. "Peter? It's your father. Would you be kind enough to take or have someone else take a photograph of the vice president nuzzling Charlene Joiner? It would be so nice to have as a souvenir. Thank you." Stone hung up. "Consider it done."

"And I know just who to e-mail it to," Ann said, "for the maximum possible effect."

S tone and Ann had a look around Ben's house, then returned to Peter's.

"I got the photograph," Peter said.

Stone gave him Ann's e-mail address, then he looked around the room. "What happened to the veep and Charlene?"

"Gone," Peter said. "I heard him tell an aide to call Spago for a table."

"Very good," Stone said.

"Very good indeed," Ann said, as she dialed a number. "The VP and Charlene Joiner will be arriving at Spago shortly," she said to whoever answered. "Greet them and e-mail me the shots." She hung up.

"Who was that?"

"A photographer acquaintance of mine," Ann said. "He

hangs around outside chic spots, waiting for celebs to show. He also has two spotters cruising the ones where he can't be and they communicate by cell phone and he rushes over on his motorcycle."

"In that case, please hold Peter's shots," Stone said. "Maybe use them later if you really need them."

"All right, I'll save my ammo."

A buffet table was operating now, and they served themselves dinner.

"I didn't get any lunch today," Ann said.

"Poor girl."

"Kate ran me off my feet. She visited four caucuses, spoke at two luncheons, and went to three cocktail parties, and she was still making 'em laugh at the end. Now she has two dinners to attend, but she excused me."

"Good Kate," Stone said, digging into his paella. A waiter brought them glasses of wine. "Are you encouraged by how things are going?" he asked Ann.

"They're going so well, it scares me," she replied. "Something's got to go wrong soon, and I hope it doesn't sneak past me."

"Not much gets past you," Stone said.

"You're catching on pretty quick, yourself," she said. "You've managed to find out what's on the governor's mind and plant lascivious things in the veep's head and it's not even eight o'clock yet."

They had just finished dinner when Immi Gotham turned up, causing heads to snap. She came and greeted Stone, who introduced her to Ann.

"We're all looking forward to your performance at The Arrington," Stone said.

"I'm looking forward to it, too," she replied. "Hattie and I have been rehearsing." Immi was stolen away by somebody.

"I like it out here," Ann said. "The quality of celebrities is better than in New York, and when they turn up, they're more relaxed. Hattie is a pianist?"

"A brilliant one. And a composer, too. She scores all of Peter's films."

"All two of them?"

"And more to come. He and Ben never stop working, and Leo Goldman is thrilled to have them on the Centurion lot. They've turned Vance Calder's old cottage into their offices." Calder, the late movie star, had been Peter's stepfather.

"How old can Peter be? Twenty-five?"

"Not that old. The boy is a prodigy."

"Does he get that from you?"

"No, and not from his mother, either. It must be some sort of genetic mutation."

"And who are Billy and Betsy Burnett?"

"That one is difficult to explain," Stone said. "Someday, when I've known you for forty or fifty years, I'll tell you the whole story. Billy is a jack-of-all-trades who has become an associate producer with Peter and Ben. He knows more about everything than anyone I know. And anyone you know, too. He can fix anything, build anything, and fly airplanes—he's been instructing Peter, Ben, and Hattie. And I wouldn't want to have him for an enemy."

"I like his wife, Betsy."

"She handles Peter's PR, schedules interviews, and makes his travel arrangements, among other things. She's made herself invaluable in the production office."

"You seem to have such a perfect life, Stone. Do you have any enemies?"

"Apparently I do," Stone said. "Last year I got into it with some Russians, out of Paris, and I thought it had ended."

"Hasn't it?"

"It seems there is an unending supply of greedy Russians. Last year they wanted The Arrington. Next year, who knows?"

Ann looked at her watch. "I know it's early, but I'm fading fast."

"Do you have a car, or do you want to ride with me?"

"I was dropped off by a campaign car. I'm with you."

They said their good nights and found The Arrington's car waiting for them out front.

They had just pulled away from the house when Ann's phone buzzed and she answered it. "Oh, look," she said, showing Stone the phone. "Marty and Charlene in Hollywoodland!"

The sidewalk in front of Spago was choked with paparazzi, and Stanton and Charlene were elbowing their way through the mob, smiles fixed on their faces, apparently enjoying themselves.

"I guarantee you," Ann said, "that picture will be on the front page of the *New York Post* tomorrow morning. And a lot of other rags, too."

S tone was having breakfast in bed with Ann the following morning when his phone rang. "Hello?"

"Stone, it's Ed Eagle. How are you?"

"I'm very well, Ed, and it's good to hear from you. Are you in Santa Fe?"

"No, I'm in L.A. for the convention. I'm a New Mexico delegate."

"When did you get in?"

"Last night. We're staying at Susannah's place in Century Center—unless you can get me something at The Arrington."

"Come and stay with me. I have an unoccupied guest room, and you haven't seen my place since it was finished. Get here in time for lunch and we'll catch up."

"I'd love to. Susannah can't make it until later—she's having a beauty day at some spa or other."

"Come at half past twelve. I'll leave your name at the gate, but prepare for a thorough pat down from a security guard."

"As long as she's beautiful," Ed said. "See you then." He hung up.

"That was my friend Ed Eagle," Stone said to Ann. "Do you know him?"

"He's a New Mexico delegate. I've seen his name on the list. Who is he?"

"A remarkable man. He was born in Brooklyn to a Hasidic Jewish family and became a fanatical basketball player in high school. His family wouldn't countenance his continuing his athletic career—they wanted him in the family diamond business—so he left the sect and got himself a basketball scholarship to Arizona State. By that time, he had grown to six feet seven inches tall. He was a great player, making all-American for three years, but he didn't play pro ball—went to law school instead. Now he lives in Santa Fe, and he's widely thought to be the best trial attorney west of the Mississippi."

"I've read something about him. Somehow, I thought he was an Indian."

"People thought that at ASU, too, and he never corrected them. It amuses him to just let people go on thinking it. Oh, and he's married to the film actress Susannah Wilde."

"She's wonderful. I love her work!"

"He had an earlier wife, though, who turned out to be a real piece of work. Let me see if I can get her story straight—there's a lot of it. Oh, yes, she's from a Jewish family, too, and she was married to an important diamond merchant who was considerably older than she. Unfortunately, she formed an attachment to a boyfriend who had a criminal streak in him and a desire to hit it big. Using information he got from her, he walked into her husband's New York offices and robbed the place of every stone in the safes. Something went wrong, and the boyfriend shot and killed her husband, then he beat it out of town without her.

"She cooperated with the police, and she was helpful in catching the guy, but she ended up doing a stretch at a women's prison in Westchester County. Ed was up there on a case, met her, and was impressed. He told her when she got out to come to Santa Fe and he'd help her restart her life. She had a couple of years left on her sentence. To his surprise, she turned up a couple of months later, having gotten out on an early-release program, and the two of them hit it off. Pretty soon they were married, and he thought it was going okay, then one day he got a call from his broker saying that she had sold most of his stock portfolio and taken all of the considerable amount of cash he had there."

"This is some story," Ann said. "If I ever write my novel . . ."

"There's more. He went to Mexico City and managed to get the bulk of his money back, then he put a couple of trackers on her to bring her back to the States. Meantime, she had killed a Mexican cop in Acapulco who had attacked her, and they got ahold of her before she could leave the country. She was sent to a women's prison east of Acapulco and within a pretty short time she had escaped and somehow made her way back to the States, where she got arrested for another murder. She was tried and, while awaiting the verdict, she escaped from the courthouse and with the help of a friend decamped to a spa somewhere around Palm Springs. It was there, a few days later, that she learned she had been acquitted at trial. At this point, all they had against her was jailbreak, and she negotiated that down to a suspended sentence."

"Is there more? I'm exhausted."

"There's more. She met and married a Silicon Valley entrepreneur who had made a billion in the electronics business. He got himself killed in a freeway accident and she inherited everything. Now she lives in San Francisco, married to a car salesman she bought a Bentley from, and she bought him the dealership. She's also inherited a significant chunk of stock in Centurion Studios.

"But all this newfound wealth has not caused her to stop hating Ed Eagle. On two occasions, she's hired hit men to kill him. Both attempts failed, but Ed lives with the knowledge that she could try again."

"What's her name?"

"She didn't change it after leaving Ed—it's still Barbara Eagle, as far as I know."

"Holy shit! I know about her. She's very big in half a dozen arts organizations in San Francisco, and she was a big Democratic contributor until someone uncovered her more unsavory aspects and Dick Collins stopped taking her money. Now she's a big-time Republican contributor!"

"As far as I'm concerned," Stone said, "they can have her."

"I want to meet Ed Eagle," Ann said.

"He's coming to lunch here today. Can you shake free?"

"I can try. Twelve-thirty, did you say?"

"Out by the pool. Susannah won't be there today, she's spa-ing."

"I'll do what I can," she said.

"I think you'll like Ed—I know he'll like you."

S tone was waiting by the pool when Ed Eagle arrived. Manolo saw to the couple's luggage, then brought a pitcher of iced tea for Stone and his guest.

"You're looking well, Ed."

"You, too, Stone. I was awfully sorry about Arrington's death."

"I got your note, thanks, and the flowers. Is Susannah well?"

"She's just great. She's been developing her own films for a while now and she enjoys that."

"She'll have to meet my son, Peter. He and Dino's son, Ben, are at Centurion now."

"I've read about him and I've seen both his films. Susannah and I were impressed."

"I'm sorry she couldn't make lunch. My girlfriend, Ann Keaton, may join us if she can get away from work."

"What does she do?"

"She's Kate Lee's deputy campaign manager, and, as you can imagine, she's pretty busy this week."

"I expect so."

"Let's give her a few minutes before we go ahead and eat," Stone said. "Tell me, what's going on with your ex-wife these days?"

"She remains a thorn in my flesh," Ed said. "I won't feel entirely safe until she's dead."

"Just don't help her along."

"It's crossed my mind," Eagle said. "Susannah would go up to San Francisco and shoot her on sight if I'd let her."

Stone laughed. "That would be even worse than doing it yourself."

"You'd think that with all the money she's got these days she would forget about me, but, no, she hasn't."

"I'm sorry to hear that."

Stone looked up to see Ann approaching, and the two men stood up. Stone introduced them and poured her a glass of iced tea.

"I'm very pleased to meet you," Ed said. "I hear you're up to your neck in Kate Lee's campaign."

"Over my head, half the time. Oh, Stone, I was right—the photograph of Marty Stanton and Charlene Joiner made the front page of the *Post*! It's also all over the West Coast papers."

"Why hasn't Stanton dropped out of the race?" Ed asked.

"We're working on it," Ann replied.

"I'd sure like to see Kate get the nomination," Ed said. "I've already sent money. Stone, I hear you were in at the beginning, among the big twenty-one contributors."

"Best money I ever spent," Stone said, "if she gets elected."

Ed looked around him. "This is certainly a beautiful place," he said. "Why don't you open an Arrington in Santa Fe?"

"Sounds like a good idea," Stone said.

"A client of mine has a little ranch for sale near Tesuque, on the outskirts of the city, that would make a good site."

"I'll speak to the board about it," Stone said. "We're opening a hotel in Paris next year with a French partner, but we haven't made another move in the States yet."

"I'd be glad to work with you if you want to come to Santa Fe. Susannah and I would invest, too."

"Let me talk to some people," Stone said.

"I've never been to Santa Fe," Ann said. "What's it like?"

"God's country," Ed said. "Seven thousand feet up in the Sangre de Cristo Mountains, beautiful climate, great restaurants and art galleries."

"We can stop there on the way home, if you like," Stone said.

"Only if we lose the nomination," Ann said. "Then I'd need somewhere to lick my wounds. But if Kate wins, then I'm going to have more on my hands than I know what to do with."

"That gives me a terrible conflict of interest," Stone said.

The phone on the table buzzed, and Stone picked it up. "Yes?"

"Mr. Bill Eggers for you, Mr. Barrington," Manolo said.

"Excuse me a minute while I take this," Stone said. He

picked up the phone and walked away from the table. "Hello, Bill?" Eggers was the managing partner of Stone's law firm, Woodman & Weld.

"Hello, Stone," Eggers said. "I know you're having too much fun out there, so I scared up some work for you."

"Gee, thanks, Bill, I'm just sitting here, having lunch with Ed Eagle, and you had to interrupt."

"Tell Ed I said hello. This could be a good client," Bill said. "A Britisher named Charles Grosvenor is making a move to Los Angeles and he wants a law firm to represent him. Word is, they're part of the London Grosvenor family, which includes the Duke of Westminster."

"You've got a dozen good lawyers in the L.A. office," Stone said.

"Your name came up—apparently he's heard of you from a friend."

"What friend?"

"I don't know, but I'd appreciate it if you'd meet with them. They're staying down the road at the Bel-Air Hotel."

"All right, I'll call them this afternoon," Stone said. "Maybe we can have a drink later in the day."

"That's good. Let me know what comes of your conversation."

"I'll do that." Stone hung up and went back to the table.

"Bill Eggers says hello, Ed. He also says I'm having too much fun out here, so he's found me some work."

"It'll be good for you," Ed said.

"We'll see."

S tone called the Bel-Air and was connected to Grosvenor's suite. A young woman with an upper-class En-
glish accent answered the phone.

"Ah, yes, Mr. Barrington," she said. "Mr. Grosvenor
is out at the moment, but he asked if you could meet him at the
Bel-Air for a drink later today."

"Of course."

"Five o'clock, in the bar, then?"

"I'll be there."

"Mr. Grosvenor looks forward to meeting you." She hung up.

THE BAR AT the Bel-Air was virtually deserted when Stone
arrived, wearing a necktie for the occasion, and he looked

around, then selected one of two chairs by the fireplace, where a small blaze lit up that side of the room. A moment later, a tall, beautifully dressed, distinguished-looking man, fiftyish, entered the room, spotted him, and walked over.

"I expect you must be Mr. Barrington," he said, smiling, "since you're the only person here."

Stone rose to greet him. "I am Stone Barrington," he said.

Grosvenor took the other chair, and Stone waved at a waitress who was loitering by the bar, waiting for business to pick up. "What may I order for you?" Stone asked as the waitress arrived.

"A Laphroaig," Grosvenor said, "no ice, please, just a little cool water."

"And a Knob Creek on the rocks," Stone said to her, and she disappeared.

"Welcome to Los Angeles," Stone said.

"Thank you. We've been here many times, of course, but we've come this time to purchase a residence and settle."

The waitress returned with their drinks, then left.

"Bill Eggers said that someone had referred you to me."

"Ah, yes, a New York friend, Emerson Wilson."

Stone had met the man at a dinner and talked with him for half the evening, but that was it. "Of course."

"I regard Emerson as a keen judge of character," Grosvenor said, "and he regards you as a good man to deal with."

"I'm flattered," Stone said. "What sort of services will you require from Woodman and Weld?"

"Perhaps you might tell me how your firm could best serve?"

"We can provide you with essential legal services, including finance and tax assessment. We can introduce you to a reputable investment adviser and a realtor to help in your search for a residence. We can also help you deal with any immigration issues you may have."

"Oh, that's not a problem for us—my wife is an American citizen."

"That makes things much simpler. Where do you currently reside, Mr. Grosvenor?"

"In Eaton Square, London, and we have a country house near Chester."

Stone recalled that Eaton Square was owned by the Duke of Westminster and that his family seat was near Chester. "And how soon do you plan to relocate?"

"You might say that, having arrived, we have already relocated. All we need is a house to complete the move."

"Have you chosen a neighborhood?"

"We quite like Bel-Air," Grosvenor said.

"You understand that I work in the New York office of Woodman and Weld and that I live in that city."

"Quite."

"There are a dozen partners in our Los Angeles offices. I think it's best that I introduce you to one of them tomorrow and that he begin to assess your needs and make recommendations."

"I was rather hoping that you could be involved."

"Of course, but I think it's best that you have an attorney on the ground in Los Angeles. I can be available in New York whenever I'm needed."

"Do you not have a residence in Los Angeles?"

"I do, at The Arrington, just up Stone Canyon, but I'm normally here only two or three times a year. I may be here more often now since my son is living here, working as a film director at Centurion Studios."

"Ah, Hollywood. That interests me."

"Well, you'll see a lot of it in Los Angeles," Stone said. "Are you available for lunch tomorrow?"

"I believe so."

"Let me invite a partner to join us who is more savvy about living in California. He will be up to date on taxes, for instance."

"Of course. What is his name?"

"I have in mind Thomas Wise, our managing partner here. He's a native Angeleno and a very knowledgeable attorney."

"May I bring Mrs. Grosvenor?"

"Of course. Would you like to have lunch in the garden here? Say, at one o'clock tomorrow?"

"That would be delightful."

Stone set down his glass, stood up, and offered his hand. "Until tomorrow at one, then."

"Good day," Grosvenor said. He left the bar, leaving Stone to deal with the check.

BACK IN THE car he phoned Tom Wise.

"Good afternoon, Stone."

"Good afternoon, Tom. I think Bill Eggers must have alerted you to the possibility of an important new client?"

"He did."

"I've made a lunch date with him and his wife for tomorrow at one in the garden at the Bel-Air."

"That's fine. Will you be joining us?"

"I will, then I'll hand off to you. His name is Charles Grosvenor, of Eaton Square, London."

"Family connection to Westminster?"

"I assume so but have no real knowledge. Perhaps you can pry it out of him."

"What's his wife's name?"

"He didn't say, but she'll be at lunch. Will your secretary book the table?"

"Of course."

"Thank you, Tom. See you tomorrow."

Stone called Eggers.

"And did you meet your new client?"

"As far as I'm concerned, he's Tom Wise's new client," Stone replied. "I told Grosvenor I'd be available for consultation from New York."

"Did that put him off?"

"Didn't seem to."

"Did he say that he was related to the Duke of Westminster?"

"No, but he did say that he lives in Eaton Square and has a country place near Chester. That puts him in the duke's neighborhood. Are you coming out for the convention?"

"Can you put me up?"

"No, I've got Dino, Mike Freeman, and Ed Eagle staying. I can try to do something at The Arrington for you."

"Okay, let me know." He gave Stone his dates.

Stone called the manager and found Eggers a suite and got him some tickets for the gala.

S tone took Dino and Viv and the Eagles to dinner in The Arrington's garden restaurant, where Ann Keaton joined them just in time to order. Stone introduced her to Ed and Susannah, Ann complimented her on her film work, and they settled in for dinner.

"I've been hearing so much about your two sons," Susannah said. "I'd love to meet them."

"I think we can arrange that," Stone said.

"I heard that they bought a novel that's a favorite of mine," she said. "*Not Far Enough*, by a Santa Fe writer, Helen Bradford."

"That's true," Stone said. "They have a script and they're going into production in a couple of weeks."

"There's a woman in the novel that I'd like to play," she

said. "It's a character part, but I have to start doing those at some point."

"When would you like to meet them?" Stone asked.

"As soon as possible. It's going to get crazy as the convention gets cranked up. How about lunch tomorrow?"

"Excuse me a moment," Stone said. He walked away from the table and called Peter. "Would you like to meet Susannah Wilde?" he asked.

"Yes, of course," Peter said. "I'm a great admirer of hers."

"Can you and Ben host her at lunch tomorrow?"

"Yes, we can do that."

"I should tell you that she's interested in playing a woman in the novel. She says it's a character part."

"God, she'd be great in the part!"

"Twelve-thirty tomorrow?"

"Yes. Can you come?"

"I have to have lunch with a new client, but you don't need me there."

"Tell her to come to the bungalow. We have a chef now."

"I'll do that. Oh, and thank you again for the party last night. I love your house—Ben's, too."

"Thanks, Dad."

Stone hung up and returned to the table. "Twelve-thirty tomorrow? They'll give you lunch at their bungalow."

"Which one?"

"It used to be Vance Calder's."

"Oh, I know it. Do you think they'll let me have a look at the script?"

"I wouldn't be surprised," Stone said.

THE FOLLOWING DAY he went back to the Bel-Air for lunch and found Tom Wise waiting for him at the table. Tom was in his early sixties but looked tan and fit.

"Just how rich are these people?" Tom asked.

"They have a house in Eaton Square, and a country place, and they want to buy in Bel-Air. If I were you, I wouldn't press them on the subject. The British upper class tend to be reticent about wealth."

"All right. If we take them on, I expect I'll find out anyway."

"I expect so."

Stone saw Charles Grosvenor approaching with a woman and he stood up to greet them. "This is Mrs. Grosvenor," he said.

"And this is Tom Wise, the managing partner of our Los Angeles office," Stone said. Mrs. Grosvenor had beautiful iron-gray hair to her shoulders, straight and parted in the middle. She appeared to be considerably younger than her husband, but they looked good together.

They sat down and ordered lunch, and Tom probed them lightly about what he could provide in the way of services.

"I think our first order of business will be an estate agent," Grosvenor said.

Tom produced a card. "This woman is the queen of Bel-Air real estate," he said. "I'll have her call you this afternoon, if that's all right."

"Of course," Grosvenor said, pocketing the card. He began

asking questions, doing the talking for both of them, and Tom responded, revealing a depth of knowledge on every subject raised. Stone hardly got a word in edgewise, but he wasn't bored. Mrs. Grosvenor seemed content to just listen. Two hours later, they parted company.

"What do you think?" Stone asked Tom as they walked to the parking lot together.

"He asks all the right questions and doesn't seem put off by the property prices in Bel-Air. He'll do for a client, I think. Did you catch the reference to his airplane?"

"I must have zoned out for a while there."

"They own a Gulfstream G450. That puts them in the stratosphere in more ways than one."

"Yes, it does," Stone said. He shook Tom's hand.

"Thanks for taking them off my hands," he said. "I doubt you'll need any help from me, but call if you do."

The two men got in their cars and left the hotel.

S tone was having a drink before dinner with the Bacchettis and Mike Freeman, waiting for the Eagles to
arrive, when the phone rang.

"Hello?"

"You son of a bitch." A woman's voice, low and threatening.
"You goddamned motherfucking bastard." The volume was
growing.

"Who is this?"

"You filthy, scum-sucking piece of shit!" She was screaming now.

"Who is this?" Stone said, then held the phone away from
his ear as the screaming continued. "Stop it!" he shouted, and
she did for a moment. "Now, let's start over. Who is this?"

"This is the best actress working in movies," she said, "the
one who's not going to get a nomination next year."

"Charlene? Is that you?"

"How could you do it?"

"Do what? What on earth are you talking about?"

"My part in Peter's picture—you gave it to Susannah Wilde, who won't have the slightest idea what to do with it!"

"I didn't give Susannah anything," Stone said. "Peter is in charge of his own work and I stay out of it."

"Then how is it that she's staying at your house and she just happened to turn up at Peter's bungalow for lunch today?"

"I set up the lunch because they both wanted to meet."

"And he gave her *my* part just like *that*! That horrible, preposterous bitch, who can't act her way out of a paper bag!"

"Charlene, you're not yourself. Let's talk another time when you can be more civil about this."

"And thank you *so much* for getting me involved with that slimy adulterer Marty Stanton."

"I didn't get you involved—you said you wanted to meet him, so I introduced you."

"And now my picture is on the front page of half the newspapers in the country with an infamous adulterer!"

"Two things, Charlene. When did you start giving a hoot about adultery? And when did you not like having your picture on the front page of half the papers in the country?"

"The whole world knows his wife just walked out on him and endorsed Kate Lee."

"The whole world including you," Stone pointed out. "He didn't take you to dinner at gunpoint, did he?"

"I'm ruined. It's all over the trades that I had the part in Peter's film."

"And who gave that to the trades?" Stone inquired. "Might it be your publicist?"

"And now fucking Susannah Wilde has the part. It's on *Entertainment Tonight* right this minute, I'm watching it. Oh, shit, they just said that Peter dumped me for her!"

"Charlene, you're behaving like a petulant child. You know how the game is played out here. You shouldn't have given that information to the trades until you'd signed a contract. Do I have to explain that to you?"

"I will never forgive you for this, Stone, never! And you tell that friend of yours Mike never to call me again!" She slammed down the phone.

Stone hung up. Everybody was staring at him.

"What was that all about?" Dino asked.

"Did I hear my name mentioned?" Mike asked.

"I'm afraid you were right, Mike, you'll never get laid again. At least not by Charlene Joiner."

"What's going on?"

"I arranged for Susannah to have lunch with Peter and Ben today, and Charlene seems to think that they offered her the part that Charlene thought she had."

"Did they?" Dino asked.

"I don't know," Stone said. He looked up to see Ed and Susannah getting out of a car and waved them over to poolside. "But I think we're about to find out."

Ed and Susannah sat down, and Manolo brought them their usuals.

"Congratulations on the new role," Stone said tentatively.

"Oh, thank you, Stone. How did you know? Did you speak to Peter?"

"No, I spoke to Charlene Joiner—or rather, she spoke to me."

"Uh-oh," Susannah said, then she grinned impishly. "Did she think she had the role?"

"So I gathered," Stone said, "between the screaming and the name-calling."

"Well, if anybody knows how this town works, it's Charlene."

"I said something to that effect to her," Stone said.

"I've always thought she didn't like me," Susannah said.

"I think that has been confirmed. And what's more, she blames me!"

"Well, you did put me together with Peter and Ben," Susannah said. "Are you upset with me?"

"No, no, not in the least. I'm happy for you and the boys. I'm just a little shaken—no woman has ever talked to me in quite that fashion."

"Don't worry about it, Stone, you just got between two actresses who wanted the same part."

"I'll make a point of never doing that again," Stone said.

Ann arrived and was given a martini. "Stone," she said tentatively, "I think we may have made a wrong move."

"What did we do?" Stone asked.

"We got Marty Stanton into the newspapers with a movie star on his arm."

"Why wasn't that a good idea?"

"Well, there was an overnight poll and Marty picked up eight points on Kate. They're tied now."

"*What?*"

"Apparently white males over thirty-five now think Marty is the greatest swashbuckler since Errol Flynn."

Ed Eagle spoke up. "From what I've heard, that's not far off the mark."

"What's the percentage of white males over thirty-five on the California delegation?" Stone asked.

"Sixty-one percent," Ann said. "And the convention opens tomorrow night."

S tone, the Eagles, and the Bacchettis were driven to the Staples Center in two Arrington SUVs. Somehow, Bentleys didn't seem appropriate for a Democratic convention. They were driven into the underground garage, where every convention ticket, skybox pass, and driver's license was checked and every one of them photographed for a convention ID, then they were admitted to a secure part of the garage by the sticker on their windshields. There were no photographers or TV cameras present here. They rode up in an elevator with an armed guard to the top of the hall. Stone had a pocketful of keys and he passed them out to the Eagles and Bacchettis. "Just in case there's a remote possibility you might want to leave the skybox." He had already given Ann her key.

They found the numbered door along a corridor, and

Stone let them inside. They entered a foyer that contained a mahogany table with a large flower arrangement on it and a number of very nice art prints on the dark green walls. There were also doors to the men's and ladies' rooms. They then walked through a set of mahogany doors into what amounted to a large living room that had been decorated by Peter's production designer at Centurion Studios.

"Can I live here, please?" Dino asked.

"Sure, Dino. There's even a shower in the men's room."

"I didn't bring a change of clothes," Dino lamented.

There was a dining table set for twelve with Wedgwood china, Baccarat crystal, and linen napkins, and a buffet table where a waiter was placing platters of canapés from the adjacent kitchen. In a corner of the room was a well-stocked bar manned by a uniformed bartender.

They were separated from the convention by an eighteen-foot-long picture window, which was mirrored on its outer side. They could see the heads of conventioneers bobble past the window; a woman stopped and checked her makeup, not realizing she was being watched from inside.

On another wall were half a dozen large flat-screen TVs tuned to the three networks, plus Fox and MSNBC. The last was tuned to a football game, in case someone got bored. There was low-volume classical music playing in the background; otherwise the room was silent. Stone picked up a remote control unit from a coffee table in front of a sofa facing the huge window and pressed a button. Suddenly, the room was filled with the noise of the convention. Some governor or other was speaking, largely ignored by the huge crowd filing to their floor seats. The governor finished, and a band began playing "Happy Days Are Here Again." Stone pressed the button again and they were back to Mozart.

A waiter materialized. "May I get anyone a drink? We have most liquors, plus wines and champagne."

Everybody ordered something. Then Ann walked into the room, followed by Molly, Kate's secretary, two Secret Service agents, and Kate herself. "Good evening, everybody," she said. "In case you are wondering why I'm here, I'm not. Candidates are not supposed to visit the convention tonight, but I couldn't resist. But the press can't find me here. And neither can my husband."

"What a nice surprise," Stone said, kissing her on the cheek. "What can we get you?"

"I think a mimosa is about my speed," Kate said. She accepted a Baccarat flute and walked over to the big window. "It's like the world's largest flat-screen TV," she said. "Stone, you've certainly made yourself comfortable here," she said. "How did you do it?"

"Peter and Ben are responsible. In case you were wondering, none of the furnishings and fittings are real. They're right out of the prop room at Centurion Studios. The electronics are rented. Only the food and drink are genuine."

A doorbell rang, surprising Stone. He went to the door and opened it to find the governor of California standing there with his wife and a plainclothes police officer. "Come in, Governor," he said, shaking hands.

"This is my wife, Cara," Dick Collins said. "Cara, Stone Barrington."

Stone took them into the big room and introduced them to the Eagles and the Bacchettis. The Collinses greeted Kate warmly, then accepted a drink from the waiter.

Stone hung back, in case they wanted to exchange confidences, but Kate waved him into the little group. "I suppose you've seen the overnight poll," she said to the governor.

"I have, but I never get excited about overnight polls. After all, opinions can change overnight, can't they?"

"I certainly hope so," Kate said.

"White males of a certain age react to sexual escapades somewhat differently from the rest of the human race," Cara Collins said.

"Never discount testosterone," Kate replied. "When are you speaking, Dick?"

"In about an hour," Collins said, checking his watch. He handed the waiter his glass, still mostly full. "I don't need that if I want to be coherent later. Just wetting the whistle." He turned back to Kate and Stone. "I had a word with Marty this afternoon. He is disinclined to accept an appointment to the Senate."

Oh, shit, Stone thought. So much for that idea.

"But that's tonight," Collins said. "Who knows what he might think tomorrow night after a fresher overnight poll comes out."

"Marty has a tendency to go where the wind blows him," Kate said.

Collins laughed. "Tell me, Kate, is there a message you'd like me to deliver?"

Kate looked at him for a moment, puzzled, then she

laughed. "I have nothing to offer Marty," she said, "unless Stone can come up with another movie star."

"I don't believe I can," Stone said.

"Then I don't suppose you know a likely porn queen?"

"I do not."

"It's just as well," Kate said. "Otherwise, we'd be awash in the testosterone of American white males over thirty-five."

Ann joined the group. "Governor, I'm hearing rumors of unrest in your delegation."

"Never believe rumors, Ann," he replied smoothly.

Everyone chatted for a while, occasionally listening to a speaker drone on.

Governor Collins stood up. "I'm afraid I must be going or they'll start getting nervous backstage."

Kate walked him to the door and, before he left, he whispered something in her ear. Kate closed the door behind him and came back into the room.

"Come on, Kate," Ann said. "What did the governor have to say?"

Kate smiled. "He said that he told Marty Stanton that his offer of the Senate seat will expire five minutes after the end of the first ballot."

Then the door opened again and the president of the United States entered the suite.

Everybody stood, and Will Lee shook every hand before sitting down.

"We weren't expecting you," Kate said to her husband.

"I wasn't coming," Will replied, "then I thought to myself, why should my wife have all the fun?" He ordered a bourbon and sat down, facing the convention floor. "I hope this is better than the football game on TV," he said.

"You must have had the press all over you downstairs," Ann said.

"No, I left the motorcade a couple of blocks up the street and arrived downstairs in a single SUV. Nobody twigged."

"Look," Ed Eagle said, pointing at a TV on the wall. They all turned and saw a shot of a single black SUV turning into the

Staples Center underground parking lot. Ed switched on the sound as Chris Matthews was saying, "We're told that was a shot of the president arriving at the convention. But there was no motorcade, and he hasn't been seen on the floor or backstage. I'm betting he's watching from a skybox." Ed switched off the sound.

"So much for my security arrangements," Will said. "If anybody calls, tell 'em I'm in some other skybox."

Mike Freeman entered the suite, shook hands with the president, and asked for a glass of orange juice.

"Have you made your rounds, Mike?" Stone asked.

"I have and all is well. Anyway, nobody would want to kill anybody who's spoken so far. I did hear a rumor that a couple of VIPs sneaked past the press into a skybox."

"Don't believe a word of it," Will said. He found the remote control and turned on the sound from the floor, plus a TV.

A documentary film began, honoring the recently deceased Senator Eleanor Stockman, and the crowd listened respectfully for five minutes, then applauded warmly.

"Here comes Dick Collins and his speech," Will said.

"And here comes the young governor of California," Chris Matthews was saying. "Eight years from now, he'll be a likely candidate for president. His first two years in office have been a spectacular success."

Dick and Cara Collins spent a couple of minutes waving at the crowd and making eye contact here and there, then finally Cara kissed him and left the platform. Then the podium and the glass shield rose from the floor.

"It worked!" Mike said. "As late as this morning we weren't sure it would."

"This is something new at a convention," Matthews was saying. "That wall of non-glare glass is said to protect against bullets, bombs, and maybe even Republicans. Also, a little inside info: you can't see it from the audience but the teleprompter is projected onto the inside of the glass wall so the speaker will appear to be speaking without reading it."

Collins began to speak. "Good evening, and welcome to the great state of California!" The crowd went suitably wild, then calmed down. "Word has reached me that a Californian is seeking your nomination." Big laugh. "I have not come here to endorse him." He waited a beat. "Nor to bury him." Another laugh. Then Collins got serious and began to speak of the challenges facing the country. He finished ten minutes later with a few short sentences. "I'm told that the current president of the United States is watching tonight. On television, of course. I want to say that this country is in the best shape it has been in for many years. Probably since World War Two. And Will Lee is the man we can thank for that!" The crowd went nuts, the band played, and Cara Collins appeared, took the governor by the hand, and led him off the stage.

"Well, that was mercifully short," Will said. "I think we can thank Bill Clinton for the brevity. And what he said about me was nice."

"Yes, but that doesn't mean it wasn't true," his wife said. "If I get this office, I'll do my best not to screw up your legacy." She took his face in her hands and kissed him.

A waiter materialized. "Ladies and gentlemen, dinner is served." They all got up and went to the table, where place cards seated Will and Kate at opposite ends of the table. The noise from the floor was turned off and the music restored.

A waiter brought a tray containing a large roast duck. He presented it, then two other waiters began to bring out plates of duck and vegetables. Stone was given the wine to taste and approve.

A cell phone was heard to buzz, and Ann left the table and went into the hallway. She came back a moment later and went to Kate. "Martin Stanton is on the phone for you. He wants a meeting."

"Not now," Kate said. "At our cottage at The Arrington." She looked at her watch. "At ten o'clock."

Ann left the room and came back a moment later. She nodded to Kate. "Done."

"Well, *that's* going to be an interesting conversation," Will said. "Who knows, maybe some history will get made."

A nn Keaton sat in the backseat of the SUV with Kate Lee as they approached The Arrington. Stone sat silently in a jump seat.

"What do you think Marty wants?" Kate asked Ann.

"I think he wants secretary of state," Ann said.

Kate turned and looked at her. "You think he's going to offer to drop out if I give him State?"

"It's my best guess," Ann said. "In those circumstances, would you give it to him?"

Kate emitted a low laugh.

KATE WENT INTO the library of the presidential cottage and looked around. There were two chairs near the fireplace and a fire had been laid. She pushed the chairs closer to the fireplace and each other, then, using a long match, lit the fire. She pulled a drinks cart closer to the chairs, then looked at her work. Fine. She heard the doorbell ring and looked at her watch. "Right on time," she murmured to herself. She opened her purse, took out a small dictating device, reset it, and pressed the record button. Then she stuck it into the outer breast pocket of her suit jacket and turned to face the door.

A butler opened the door. "The vice president, Madame Director," he said.

Martin Stanton swept into the room, his hand outstretched. "Kate, how are you? It's been too long."

Kate took it and allowed him a peck on her cheek. "Last month isn't so long ago," Kate said. "Have a seat, Marty. Can I get you a cognac?"

"Yes, thank you." Stanton went and stood in front of a chair but did not sit down until she had poured the drinks, handed him a glass, and sat down herself. I can't fault his manners, Kate thought.

"I want to have a serious talk with you, Kate," Stanton said. "We're coming into this convention with me in the lead and you trailing everybody else."

"I watch the news, too, Marty," she said, keeping any reproof from her voice. "And what I'm hearing is that you're short of the votes you need for the nomination."

"I'm here to tell you—all that has changed," Marty said. "The California delegation is solid for me, and I've heard only this evening from nineteen delegates from other states who will switch their votes to me."

"On which ballot, Marty?" Kate asked, trying to sound really curious.

"Why, the first ballot, of course. I know you've been counting on a second ballot, with all the delegates free to change their votes to you, but that simply isn't going to happen."

"You may be right," Kate said, "but on the other hand—"

"There is no other hand, Kate. I now have the nomination in my pocket."

"Is that what you came to tell me?"

"Not entirely," Stanton said. "I've come to ask you to be my secretary of state."

"That's awfully generous of you, Marty."

"You're perfectly suited for it. I've always thought of director of Central Intelligence as a foreign policy post."

"So have I," she replied.

"There's nobody in the party who can lay a glove on you for qualifications."

"I appreciate the compliment. And what do *you* want, Marty?"

"Me?" As if the thought of a quid pro quo had never occurred to him.

"There must be something."

"Well, I think it would be very good for the party and the country if you nominated me tomorrow night. It would bring us together better than anything I can think of."

"And whom were you thinking of for your running mate?"

"I think the senior senator from Pennsylvania," Stanton said. "With Pete Otero, we'd have two westerners as running mates. I think an easterner would be better for the ticket."

That, Kate thought, is the worst possible ticket I can think of. "I'm sure your reasoning is sound, Marty."

"And with you in the wings, waiting to take over at State, well, that would be like having another running mate."

"You'd announce me for State before the general election?"

"I don't think that would be presumptuous, given your stature."

"Did you consider a woman as a running mate?" she asked coyly.

Stanton took a sip of his drink. "If you'll forgive my saying so, Kate," he said, "I think that perhaps since the country has had a Lee in office for eight years, it might be a bit of an overdose to have you as number two for another eight."

"Did it ever occur to you that they might not have had enough of the Lees?"

"They love you both, Kate, but they're not addicted. You have to be realistic."

Kate smiled but said nothing.

"What about it, Kate? Will you come with us?"

"Marty, I will make you a pledge right now."

"And what is that?"

"I will support the nominee of my party."

Stanton set his glass down on the little table next to his chair. "Well, I'm disappointed that you won't accept, Kate, but I'll give you until noon tomorrow to think about it. Talk it over with Will."

"Oh, I'll do that," Kate said. She waited for him to stand, then she did, too. She held out her hand. "Thank you for coming to see me, Marty," she said.

"Good night, Kate. I hope to hear from you tomorrow."

"You will, Marty." She watched him go, closing the door behind him. She heard the outside door close and a car door slam, then she switched off her pocket recorder, picked up the phone, and pressed a button. "Come on in," she said.

The door opened and Ann and Stone entered the room.

"Pull up another chair, Stone," she said, "and pour us all another cognac, will you, please?"

Stone carried out his instructions and sat down.

Nobody said anything for a moment.

"Well?" Ann asked, unable to contain herself.

"*He* offered *me* State," she said.

Ann laughed out loud. "The arrogant son of a bitch!"

"He says he wants 'the senior senator from Pennsylvania' for a running mate."

"The worst possible combination," Ann said.

"Funny, I thought exactly the same thing."

"Did he say anything else of import?"

"I believe he did," Kate said, "though it wasn't his intent to say it."

"What?"

Kate smiled. "He doesn't have the votes to win on the first ballot."

S tone and Ann walked back to his house together. "Kate takes my breath away," he said.

"Mine, too," Ann replied.

"Do you think she's right about Stanton not having the votes to win on the first ballot?"

"Kate doesn't make pronouncements that aren't hedged in some way—'in my opinion,' 'it's my guess that . . .' et cetera."

"But she just did."

"She did, didn't she?"

"She must feel very certain, then."

"She must, mustn't she?"

"But you aren't?"

"I honestly don't know. I've just rarely heard her make flat-footed statements like that."

"Does she know something you don't know?"

"Sam Meriwether is in charge of counting delegates," Ann said. "He hasn't shared anything like that with me."

"I'll tell you something," Stone said, "I've never had more fun in my life than watching all this happen."

"Maybe you should run for office, Stone."

"Ha! And give up life as I know it?"

Ann laughed. "Life as you know it is pretty good, isn't it?"

"It's spectacular! Being on the inside of the action and having you in my bed every night is almost more than I can stand."

Ann laughed again. "It's almost more than I can stand, too."

"What are you going to do if Kate wins?"

"Just between you and me?"

"Of course."

"I'm going to be the next White House chief of staff."

"Kate has offered you that?"

"She has, and I've accepted."

"What is that going to do to your life?"

"It will destroy my life as I know it," Ann said. "I'll be constantly on call—twenty-four/seven—I won't get much sleep. And I won't have a social life that doesn't involve a White House dinner."

"That doesn't sound very good for you and me," Stone said.

"No, it doesn't—you're going to have to give me up if Kate is president."

"Entirely?"

"Oh, we can have an occasional dinner and roll in the hay, in D.C. or New York. But for every four dates we make, I'll have to break three. Something will come up."

"I don't like the sound of that much."

"I don't like it much, either," Ann said, "but it's how it will be. I'll have a chance to make a difference for this country, and I'll give up everything else to do that."

"I can't blame you, Ann."

"Thank you."

"What will you do if Kate loses?" he asked.

"I'll move to New York, apply for a job with Woodman and Weld, and sleep with you every night. If you'll have me."

"No doubt about that."

"You're sweet."

"I'm greedy."

"It's one of the things I like best about you," she said. "Let's go be greedy right now."

And they did.

HALF A MILE down Stone Canyon, Mr. and Mrs. Charles Grosvenor were undressing after dinner.

"How did you think our lunch went?" Charles asked his wife.

"I thought it went very well."

"Do you think Barrington recognized you?"

"I know he didn't," she said. "I've always been good at makeovers."

"You certainly have—and I love the gray hair."

"I thought of affecting a British accent, but that might have been a little much. After all, there are people in L.A. who know who Barbara Eagle Grosvenor is."

"What if Barrington mentions our lunch to Ed Eagle? He knows my name."

"He won't have any reason to mention it, since he hasn't figured it out."

"And you're going to use Barrington to get at Eagle?"

"Ideally, yes. Don't worry, I won't get caught. I'll get away with it, I always have."

"You have that gift," Charles said. "And what will you do if you can't get at Eagle?"

Barbara smiled a little smile. "Then I'll destroy someone close to him."

"Barrington?"

"Perhaps. It would cut Ed to the bone, and that's been my pleasure for a long time."

"Whatever you want, my sweet."

"I want you to come over here and fuck me," she said, stretching out on the bed.

"It's what I do best, isn't it?" he asked, joining her.

"It certainly is, my darling."

19

*G*overnor Richard Collins was joined for breakfast by Vice President Martin Stanton in the governor's bungalow at the Beverly Hills Hotel. A table had been elegantly laid on the private patio. The governor was sitting in a chaise longue, reading a stack of morning papers. A political writer's daily column had caught his eye, and he read it quickly.

"Good morning, Dick," the vice president said from the patio door. A Secret Service agent stood behind him. The agent looked quickly around the patio, then stepped back into the bungalow's living room and closed the door between him and his charge.

"Good morning, Marty," Collins said, rising to greet his guest. "Shall we sit down?" He motioned his guest to a chair. "Orange juice?" the governor asked, picking up a pitcher.

"Thank you, yes."

"Would you like some champagne or vodka in it?"

"Thanks, I'll wait until lunchtime."

Collins poured the orange juice, and a waiter came and delivered eggs Benedict. "So, Marty, how do you think the convention is going for you?"

"As well as can be expected," Stanton replied.

"Do you think you have enough votes to win on the first ballot?"

Stanton hesitated before replying. "I believe that may depend on you, Dick."

Collins took a bite of his eggs and shrugged. "I think our delegation is holding. At least, nobody has told me he's doing otherwise."

"I hear rumors that there's some crumbling in Pete Otero's delegation."

"You mean, some of his delegates are switching to you?"

"I mean, I hear they're switching—I can't be sure to whom."

"I hear there may be half a dozen," Collins said.

"Do you hear where they're going?"

"I can only guess."

"All right then, guess."

"I think more likely to Kate than to you."

"That won't hurt me on the first ballot," Stanton said.

"No, that won't, not until the second ballot."

"Then we'll have to wait and see, won't we?"

The governor chewed thoughtfully. "How did your sit-down with Kate go last evening?"

Stanton flinched visibly. "How could you know about that?"

"I try to stay on top of things. What did you two have to say to each other?"

"She offered me State if I'd drop out and nominate her."

"If you don't get the nomination, Marty, which would you prefer, State or the Senate?" Collins already knew the answer. State was too much work, too much globe-hopping for Stanton, who had always been a little lazy.

"I guess that's my choice, isn't it? If I don't win the nomination."

"What did you say to Kate?"

"After I turned it down, I offered her State."

"And?"

"She wouldn't commit—said she'd let me know by noon."

"Marty, it's time for you and I to be entirely honest with each other. Realistic, too."

"How do you mean?"

"Kate isn't going to take State."

"I've got until noon before we know."

"It's not going to happen. Put it out of your mind."

"I don't see how you can know that, Dick."

"You'll know at noon, but by then you will have wasted four hours."

"Wasted how?"

"You have no time to waste, Marty. Right now, you can accept my offer of an appointment to the Senate. That offer will expire when we rise from this table. Then, when Kate calls you at noon—or, more likely, doesn't call at all—you will be out of options."

"But you said—"

"No, I didn't," Collins said. "I didn't say my offer was open-ended. And Kate didn't offer you State."

Stanton's shoulders slumped. "I don't see how you can say that, Dick, you weren't there."

"I didn't need to be."

"Why not?"

"Because I know you, Marty, and I know Kate. The fact is, your personal conduct has made it impossible for you to be nominated."

"I know it hasn't helped," Stanton admitted.

"In the Senate, Marty, no one will care who you take to bed, you'll be a bachelor again. You're rich enough to buy a nice house in Georgetown—the women will be all over you. Think about it."

"I'll have no seniority in the Senate."

"Your stature in the party will get you good committee assignments, and the press will always want to know what you have to say, especially the TV reporters. You'll be a regular on the Sunday-morning shows."

"Do you know something I don't, Dick? About who's slipping in the delegation?"

"Nobody has told me anything, I just know what I know. It's time for you to decide what you want to do with the rest of your life. You can spend it doing good work in the Senate, or you can spend it serving on corporate boards and playing golf."

"Come on, Dick, I've done a lot for you. You wouldn't be governor—"

"And I'm very grateful to you, Marty, that's why I've offered you the Senate seat. Most politicians would kill for that."

The governor finished his eggs. Stanton hadn't touched his. Collins looked at his watch. "Well, I've got a nine-o'clock across town." He pushed his chair back.

"Time to decide, huh?" Stanton said.

"Yes, it is, Marty."

Stanton pushed his chair back and stood up. "All right, Dick, I'll take the Senate seat."

Collins stood up and shook his hand. "Wonderful, Marty, and I'll be there when you run for reelection in four years."

"Thank you, Dick."

"Now," said the governor, taking Stanton's arm and propelling him toward the door, "let me tell you how this is going to go."

The two men walked slowly through the bungalow's living room and outside to where their cars waited. The governor did all the talking; Stanton nodded. At one point, Stanton seemed to object, but Collins kept him moving, talking earnestly in a low voice.

They reached their cars, and a Secret Service agent was holding the door open for Stanton.

"Then we're agreed, Marty." It wasn't a question.

Stanton nodded, got into the car, and was driven away. Collins did the same, but he was smiling.

A nn Keaton sat at her desk in her small office in the presidential cottage and began working delegates, one by one. Molly, Kate's secretary, sat at an adjacent desk. Her phone rang, she listened and then tapped Ann on the shoulder.

Ann covered the phone. "Yes, Molly?"

"Hang up."

"I'll call you back," Ann said into her phone, then hung up.

"Evan Chandler, from Senator Mark Willingham's campaign, wants to speak to you," Molly said. "This could be important."

Ann pressed the button. "Good morning, Evan, how are you?"

"Very well, Ann. Senator Willingham would like to meet with Director Lee—this morning, if possible."

"She has meetings all morning and a lunch at twelve thirty," Ann said. "I could make some time between the meetings and lunch—say, twelve?"

"That's fine. The senator would like to meet in his suite at the Bel-Air."

"I'm afraid that won't be possible, given her schedule," Ann said. "It will have to be at the presidential cottage at The Arrington."

"Hold on."

Ann found herself listening to piano music.

"What's going on?" Molly asked.

"I'm on hold. Willingham wants a meet, but I won't let the first lady go to him."

"Ann?" Chandler was back on the line.

"Yes, Evan."

"The senator will be there at noon."

"I'll leave word at the gate," Ann said. "Security is very tight here."

"He'll be on time." Chandler hung up.

Ann put down the phone and ran down the hall to the presidential office. She rapped on the door and opened it. Kate and Will Lee were sitting on the sofa, their laps full of papers.

"Director, you have a meeting with Mark Willingham at noon, here."

"I do?" Kate asked, surprised.

"Unless you want me to cancel."

Will looked at her and shook his head.

"All right, Ann."

Ann smiled and went back to her desk.

KATE LOOKED AT WILL. "Now, what do you suppose?"

"It won't be State," Will said.

"He's not going to offer me the number two spot," Kate said.

"Why not? Mark will do whatever he has to do, and he's all out of time. Nominations are tonight, and he'll want to have everything lined up. He obviously believes that Marty doesn't have the votes to win on the first ballot."

"It's incongruous," Kate said. "Willingham was your worst enemy among the Democrats in the Senate."

"Doesn't matter. Mark has decided you're the only way he can win."

Kate shook her head. "Impossible."

"Well," Will said, "all you have to do is listen."

KATE HAD ARRANGED the furniture again in the library and was sitting when the knock came.

"Senator Willingham," Manolo said.

Willingham strode into the room and shook Kate's hand, then sat down. He didn't wait for her to sit first.

"What can I do for you, Senator?" Kate asked.

"I have it on good authority that the California delegation is cracking," he said.

"Cracking how?" Kate asked.

"On the first ballot, after California votes, someone will ask the chair to poll the delegation."

"How much of a crack are we talking about?"

"A dozen, fifteen votes."

"And whom will they crack for?"

"Me."

"So that will give you, what, ninety, ninety-five delegates to the vice president's one twenty, one twenty-five?"

"My people think that when California cracks, delegates from other states will start to jump ship. They think I've got a very good shot at a first-ballot win. And if it goes to a second ballot, we're a sure thing."

"That's awfully optimistic of you, Senator," Kate said.

"I know it is, that's why I'm here. I want you to nominate me tonight. I think that could make the difference."

"Well, I suppose there's a weird kind of logic to that idea," Kate said. "Of course, when delegates start to jump, many might go to Otero. And as strange as it may seem to you, Senator, many of them might even go to me."

"Kate, would the vice presidency appeal to you?"

"Senator, is that an offer?"

"I'm just curious."

"Satisfying your curiosity is not very appealing to me, Senator."

"All right, if you'll nominate me tonight, the vice presidency is yours."

"Senator, the vice presidency is not yet your gift to give."

"You know what I mean—you'll have the number two spot on the ticket with me."

"Shall I be frank with you, Senator?"

"By all means."

"I don't think California can crack enough to give you the nomination. I don't think that enough ship jumpers would go to you, either. In fact, if suddenly Marty dropped out of the race, I don't think you'd get the nomination."

A flash of anger passed across the senator's face and he stood up. "I'll take that as a no," he said.

"That's very perceptive of you," Kate replied.

"Good day." He stalked across the room and out the door.

Ann came into the room. "He looked very angry, Director. Did you tell him to go fuck himself?"

"Pretty much," Kate replied.

S tone hosted Kate and Ann for lunch on his poolside
patio. Ann had billed it as a strategy session.

"Whew!" Kate said, blowing upward to clear her
forehead of a strand of hair.

"Is Ann working you too hard?" Stone asked.

"When Will was running I met a lot of people, but that was
nothing compared to now. I'm having to soak my hand in ice
water to keep the swelling down."

"How do you feel about the way things are going?" Stone
asked.

"If all I needed was the goodwill of the delegates I've met,
I'd feel very confident," she said. "Unfortunately, I'm not the
only one seeking their votes and most of them are already
committed, barring a second ballot."

"If you had it to do over, would you start earlier and enter the primaries?"

Kate thought about it. "No, I don't think so. I think I've done the right thing almost by accident."

"How by accident?"

"I had thought about doing it last year and going through the whole process and decided against it. Then, months later, over dinner, Will said something to me about it not being too late. I had been thinking about life after the White House. And if Will hadn't said that at that moment, it wouldn't have occurred to me that I might have a chance if I got in late."

"What did he say?"

"He said the field had been narrowed to three candidates and all of them were making credible showings, so the chances of one of them winning on the first ballot were slim."

"He didn't think at that point that Marty Stanton would make it?"

"He thought Marty could, but he also thought there was a very good chance that he'd get caught with his pants down and implode. Well, he got caught, but the implosion isn't complete yet, so he could still win."

"What does Sam Meriwether think the count is?"

"Marty needs a hundred and thirty-five delegates out of two seventy to win on the first ballot and he has about a hundred and thirty-two. Willingham has about eighty-one and Otero has maybe fifty."

"And how many do you have, Kate?"

"We're figuring none."

"But surely—"

"Most of the people who would vote for me on the first ballot are from primary states and are committed to the man who won their states, and by the time I got in, the others were pretty much committed. Sam thinks it's better if we work on a worst-case basis, and that's no delegates for me. I've no chance unless Marty fails to get a hundred and thirty-five. Then we'll see."

"I have to admit," Stone said, "it seems impossible."

"That's what we want everybody to think," Ann said, "until tomorrow night."

"Well, yes."

"Pete Otero hasn't called you," Ann said. "I find that odd that he wouldn't want your support."

"Pete knows he isn't going to win the nomination, so he doesn't need my support," Kate said. "I'm sure that both Marty and Willingham have already met with him and I expect they've both offered him the vice president's slot on the ticket. He's smart not to commit. If he made the wrong move, then he'd miss eight years of being vice president, then a really good shot at the presidency. And if whoever gets the nomination loses in the general, Pete is first in line for the nomination four years from now. Remember Jack Kennedy at the 1956 election? He thought he'd get the vice president slot on the ticket, but Adlai Stevenson threw him a curve ball when he threw the vice presidential nomination open to the convention and Estes Kefauver won. But by that time Jack was as well known to the electorate as almost anybody in the party, and when Adlai lost, the nomination was wide open to him in 1960. Pete has patience and it may work well for him."

They ate their lunch talking mostly about everything but the convention. Stone saw Kate relaxing and he thought the change of subject probably did her good.

THEY WERE DONE with lunch and on coffee when the telephone buzzed and Stone answered.

"Telephone for Mrs. Lee," Manolo said.

"Who's calling?"

"They wouldn't say."

Stone pressed the hold button. "Mystery call for you, Kate. Do you want to take it?"

"Who would know you were here?" Ann said.

"Let's find out," Kate replied. She took the phone and pressed the button. "Kate Lee. Good morning—or afternoon, as it may be." She listened for a moment. "All right, I agree—not even Will." She listened some more. "How sure are you about this? Thank you for calling." She hung up.

No one said anything for a long moment.

"Who was it?" Ann asked finally.

"I'm sorry, I can't say," Kate said. She drank the last of her coffee. "Will you excuse me, please? I think I want to go and lie down for a little while. And, Ann, please cancel the rest of today's schedule."

Ann's face fell. "Are you sure?"

"I don't think it will matter," Kate said and got to her feet. They stood with her.

"Thank you so much for lunch, Stone," she said, then she walked toward the presidential cottage, and the two Secret Service agents standing a few yards away fell in a few paces behind her.

"What do you suppose that was all about?" Stone asked.

"I have absolutely no idea," Ann replied. "Did you see her face? It had to be bad news if she canceled her schedule. She had half a dozen appointments with delegates this afternoon."

"She certainly didn't seem elated."

"Somehow," Ann said, "I have the feeling that the bottom has just dropped out of her world."

T he convention opened at two P.M. and would finish in the early evening to allow for various scheduled events around town, including the fund-raiser in The Arrington's amphitheater. The last two hours of the day were devoted to nominating speeches, one for each candidate. Stone didn't bother to take his group to the hall; they could watch the speeches on TV, if they chose to, and have plenty of time to dress for the evening.

Stone spent the early part of the afternoon reading, and close to five o'clock Ann found him in his study.

"You through early?" Stone asked.

"Yes, with Kate's schedule canceled I had little to do. I thought I would watch the nominating speeches with you."

"Sounds exciting." Stone switched on the TV. "Who's nominating Kate?"

"Bob Marcus, the junior senator from Georgia. He'll be last."

They watched as a Virginia congressman nominated Mark Willingham. From what Stone knew of Willingham, he hardly recognized the man described in the nomination speech.

A Colorado senator nominated Pete Otero, and much was made of the importance of the Hispanic vote in the general election.

"Is Kate watching?" Stone asked.

"I'm not sure, she was sleeping earlier, which is unlike her, but there's a TV in the bedroom. Marty's is next, and Governor Collins is nominating him."

The convention chairman approached the podium and hammered for order. "Fellow delegates," he shouted, "we have a change in our program. Ladies and gentlemen, the vice president of the United States."

"Oh, God," Ann said, "what is this? It's completely out of order for Marty Stanton even to be in the hall, let alone speak!"

"He must be desperate," Stone said.

"Look at those faces," Ann said, pointing at the people on the floor of the convention. "They're as baffled as I am."

The vice president approached the podium, wearing a dark suit and a broad smile. He waited for the applause to die but didn't try to suppress it, then he began.

"Mr. Chairman, delegates to the convention, honored guests, ladies and gentlemen," he intoned. "I beg your indulgence for having requested to speak to you at this time and I thank Senator Robert Marcus of Georgia and Governor Richard Collins for yielding the platform to me. For many months

I have been traveling this great country, speaking, debating, and, along the way, meeting most of you, and I have articulated my vision for the future of our country to the nation at large. I haven't done quite as well as I had hoped." This was followed by a shocked noise from the delegates.

Ann sat up in her chair. "Jesus," she said, "he's pulling out! He's going to throw the nomination to Willingham!"

"That must be the news Kate got at lunch," Stone said.

"It couldn't have been anything else. No wonder she was so devastated."

Stanton went on. "After long thought, much prayer, and some very good advice from some very good friends, I have decided not to seek the nomination of my party."

The audience reaction was a mixture of *Nooo*s, cheers, and general shock.

Chris Matthews's voice-over came on. "That's it," he said, "the nomination is going to Willingham. This is completely unexpected. We all thought that Stanton would fight to the last delegate. He must have had some very bad news."

Stanton continued. "I have also given a great deal of thought to my next step," he said, "and I have decided to throw my support—and ask those delegates pledged to me to throw their support—to the candidate I know, from my personal experience, is supremely well qualified to lead our party to victory in the November election. My fellow Americans, it is my honor and privilege to place in nomination the next president of the United States, Katharine Lee!"

The audience went nuts, the band started to play, and people with Kate Lee signs were, apparently spontaneously, marching up and down the aisles. Only the Virginia and New Mexico delegations sat in shocked silence.

Ann pressed the speaker button on the phone on the table between Stone and her and dialed a number.

"Hello?" a sleepy voice said.

"Kate, wake up. Turn on the TV."

"I'm awake and the TV is on."

"Did you know about this?"

"I'm sworn to secrecy. I couldn't even tell Will. Uh-oh, I hear Will running up the stairs. Talk to you later!" She hung up.

"Did you hear that?" Ann said.

"I did," Stone replied.

"I'm overwhelmed," Ann said. "I can't believe this is happening."

"I think I see the fine hand of Dick Collins in this," Stone said. "I'll bet he took Stanton aside and demolished his hopes. I wonder how he did that."

"I can guess," Ann said. "I think he must have told Marty that a bunch of the California delegates were going to jump ship on the first ballot—and he may just have told him that his offer of the Senate seat was about to expire. Marty wouldn't have had the guts to brazen it out through the first ballot and negotiate later."

"Shouldn't you go and see Kate?" Stone asked.

"No, she's with Will. I don't want to bust in on that. I'd better start making some calls, though. Do you mind if I do it here?"

"Go right ahead," Stone said.

Ann's cell phone rang. "Hello? Oh, Governor Otero, how are you? I'm sure she'd like to speak to you, but she and the president are sequestered at the moment. May I have her call you back a little later in the afternoon? Thank you for your patience." She hung up. "I think that makes it official," she said. "Pete Otero wants the number two spot and he's going to be willing to trade his delegates for it."

"Kate has already said he would be her first choice," Stone said.

"I think we're seeing history being made," Ann said, then started making calls.

23

A nn finished her calls and hung up.

"Now what?" Stone asked.

"Now I go see Kate. Come with me."

"All right." Stone got up and followed her out of the house and across the back lawn and the road to the presidential cottage.

Ann looked around the ground floor and returned. "She's still upstairs with Will," she said. "Let's wait in the library." She led the way.

Stone took a seat on a sofa while Ann fielded calls on her cell phone, mostly from the press. "I didn't know about it until it happened," she said to one reporter. "No plans for a press conference now. You'll be notified." She hung up. "That was a typical conversation," she said, switching off her phone before it rang again. They could hear the phones ringing in the office next door. Ann went in there, then came back. "Molly's got it under control," she said.

"Why don't you have a seat and take a breath," Stone said, patting the sofa next to him. "Would you like a drink?"

"I would," said a voice from the door. "So would I," said another.

They looked up to see the first lady and the president, closing the door behind them.

Ann ran to hug Kate, and Stone stood up. "Congratulations, Kate," he said, pecking the offered cheek. He shook Will's hand, too. Then he went to the bar and filled everyone's order. Finally, they were seated.

"Governor Otero called," Ann said. "He wants to meet."

"I don't want to see him," Kate said.

"Then will you call him? I think it would be a good idea."

"Then get him on the phone, please."

Ann dialed the number on the phone nearest Kate and handed it to her. She pressed the speaker button and set the phone down.

"This is Pete Otero," a man's voice said.

"Hello, Governor, it's nice of you to call," Kate replied.

"I wanted to congratulate you, Director. I don't know how this happened, but whatever you did, it was effective."

"I myself am not sure how it happened," Kate said, "but I expect someone will tell me pretty soon."

"Director, I'm at your disposal," Otero said. "What would you like me to do?"

"Governor, I think the best thing to do is to continue to follow the published schedule of the convention and hold the balloting tomorrow night. I expect we're all curious to find out what the delegates do."

"Are you going to choose a running mate before then?" the governor asked.

"No, Governor, I'm not. I don't want to get into the business of trading appointments for ballots. I want to see how the voting goes and, if I'm nominated, then I'll consider my options."

"I understand completely," Otero said.

"Would you and your wife like to be my guests at the fundraiser at The Arrington tonight?"

"We had planned to attend and we'd be delighted to join you."

"I'll see you then." Kate said goodbye and hung up. "Ann, will you call Mark Willingham's campaign manager and Marty Stanton and ask them to join me in my box tonight? I invited Governor and Mrs. Collins a couple of days ago."

"I'll see that the furniture is arranged correctly in the box," Stone said.

Kate found a sheet of paper and made some notes, then handed it to Stone. "Here's the seating plan. I'd like the seats marked with the names."

Stone looked at the sheet. Will was on one side of Kate, he and Ann were on the other. The Bacchettis and the Eagles were on the far side of Will, and the Collinses, Stanton and guest, the Willinghams, and the Oteros were in the row behind.

Stone went and called the hotel manager, faxed him the seating plan, then returned to the library. Sam Meriwether had arrived and made himself a drink.

"Sam," Kate said, "what do you expect in the balloting?"

"Are you going to pick a running mate before then?" the senator asked.

"No. I told Otero I didn't want to get into swapping jobs for delegates and that seemed fine with him."

"My people are calling every delegate now," he said. "We should have an estimate within the hour."

"Director," Ann said, "can you tell us now who was on the phone with you at lunchtime?"

"I suppose I can now," Kate said. "It was Dick Collins."

"Did he tell you how all this came to pass?"

"He didn't. He just told me that Marty was going to nominate me." She turned to Will. "I'm sorry I couldn't tell you— Dick swore me to secrecy."

"He did a great job of keeping it under his hat," Sam said. "It's my bet that only he, Marty, and you knew what was going to happen. I'll bet the chairman didn't know until it was Dick's turn to speak."

"It's my guess," Ann said, "that the governor took the vice president aside and told him that some California delegates were going to jump to you and that the offer of the Senate appointment was expiring."

"If he did, that was a masterful move," Kate said. "Dick never even told me what he was going to do after the first ballot. If that's what happened, then I'm very impressed with him. Stone, what was your impression of him at your meeting at Peter's house?"

"Calm and entirely in control," Stone said. "That was quite a contrast with the vice president when I spoke to him later.

I've always liked Collins. I'm impressed with his record and now I admire him."

"That pretty much speaks for me, too," she said.

A phone call came for Sam Meriwether and he took it outside the room. He came back five minutes later. "Our head count put us with a hundred and eleven delegates for Kate—that's the great majority of the vice president's count—sixty-nine for Willingham, and fifty-seven for Otero. About forty-three are undecided. I'd say we're looking very good." Another call came for him and he left again.

"You're going to have to get a majority of the undecideds," Will said to Kate. "It may not happen on the first ballot."

Sam Meriwether returned. "That was Dick Collins. Ann, your take on what Dick did was right on the money. He's now personally calling all the undecideds in the California delegation. There are fifteen or so."

"Let's hope he swings them all," Will said. "That will make it a lot easier for Kate."

Kate stood up, and everyone stood up with her. "Let's all go and get ready for tonight," she said.

S tone and Ann were getting dressed for the gala when Manolo buzzed him for a phone call.

"Mr. Barrington, that fellow from the Secret Service is on line one."

"Thank you, Manolo." Stone pressed the button. "Hello?"

"Mr. Barrington, this is Secret Service Special Agent Mervin Beam."

"Good evening, Agent Beam."

"Good evening. I'm in the hotel manager's office, and he tells me that you have rearranged the seating plan for your box at tonight's performance. Is that correct?"

"That is correct."

"I'm afraid that won't do," Beam said. "I had previously done a seating plan for security reasons, and I must insist that you return to that plan."

"Agent Beam," Stone said, "the seating plan I faxed to the hotel manager was drawn up by Mrs. Lee herself. It was done carefully and thoughtfully, and I suggest that you conform your security arrangements to her seating plan."

"I'm afraid it's just not secure."

"I'm afraid I don't understand how a seating plan in a theater box could be insecure because of the seating plan," Stone said, "and I'm sure Mrs. Lee will feel the same way."

"Then I'll take it up with her," Beam said.

"I wouldn't advise that. It looks as though your relationship with Mrs. Lee may very well continue until at least the first Tuesday in November, and perhaps for another four years beyond that, perhaps even eight. This would not be a good time for her to begin to view your command of her detail in an unfavorable light."

Beam was silent for a long moment. "I'm sorry to have disturbed you. The seating plan will be as Mrs. Lee wishes."

"Thank you, Agent Beam, and good evening." Stone hung up.

"What was that all about?" Ann asked, motioning Stone to zip up the back of her dress.

"Agent Beam," Stone replied. "He's upset that Kate changed the seating arrangements in our box. He thinks the new plan is insecure."

"I don't understand," Ann said.

"Neither do I, and neither, I think, does Agent Beam."

"He's a peculiar man," Ann said, "somehow different from the other agents, who are always so helpful. Beam always wants things done his way."

"He has a big responsibility, I suppose, but he could handle it better. Do you have any say in Kate's dealings with Beam's office?"

"Only as a bearer of messages."

"Why don't you ask Kate to speak to the chief of the Secret Service and request that Beam be replaced?"

"I don't think she would do that," Ann said. "She tries hard not to be pushy when dealing with the Service."

"Who else would be able to get a change made?"

"Well, the president, of course, but I don't think it's my place to speak to him about it."

Stone nodded and tied his black bow tie.

"You do that very smoothly," Ann said.

"I saw a movie once in which Cary Grant tied his bow tie that way and I practiced for hours until I got it right."

Ann collapsed in laughter.

THEY WENT DOWNSTAIRS and joined the Eagles and the Bacchettis for a drink while they waited for the president and first lady to join them for the ride to the amphitheater in an articulated electric tram.

When Stone got a chance, he pulled Dino aside. "You're acquainted with Special Agent Beam, aren't you?"

"Yeah, we've met. And he's always hanging around, watching his agents."

"You remember the threat that Beam received in an e-mail?"

"Yeah."

"I spoke with an expert about this and he said that the

e-mail almost certainly originated inside the L.A. Secret Service office."

"And what did you make of that?" Dino asked.

"Nothing, until a few minutes ago. I had a strange phone call from Beam about tonight's seating plan." He told Dino about the conversation.

"You think Beam thinks there might be a move against Kate tonight?"

"I don't know, but he was pretty upset about his seating plan being changed to Kate's seating plan."

"Do you want to mention it to somebody?"

"Who would I mention it to? Beam? We've already talked. And he's in charge of the detail, after all."

"I see your point."

"Are you armed?" Stone asked.

"Always," Dino replied. "You?"

"No."

"Why don't you run upstairs and take care of that?"

"I'll be right back." Stone ran lightly up the stairs, went into the master suite, opened the safe, and took out his little Colt Government .380. He slipped it into the lightweight shoulder holster, shoved a magazine into the pistol, racked the slide and set the safety, then tucked the weapon under his arm.

When he got back to the library, the president and first lady had arrived, and they were called to board the tram for the trip to the amphitheater.

They moved out. Four Secret Service agents trotted alongside the tram, and Special Agent Mervin Beam brought up the rear in a golf cart.

T he tram arrived at the rear of the amphitheater and everyone got off and walked through a door directly into Stone's box. It was at the very rear of the theater, and this tier was the only one with a roof, but it was open to the amphitheater.

Beam held the door open for them and they filed into the box and found their seats, which had been labeled with their names. Stone was the last through the door and he noticed that even though it was a cool desert evening, Agent Beam was sweating heavily. As Stone stepped into the box, Beam followed him and closed the door behind him. Stone heard a lock being turned and as he glanced back he saw Beam slip a key into his jacket pocket. The front of the man's shirt was now showing big sweat stains as the shirt stuck to his body.

As he took his seat, Ann pulled a stole around her shoulders. "Chilly, isn't it?" she asked.

"It is," Stone said, and he looked back at Beam again. The agent was standing, leaning against the door, sweat pouring down his face. He unbuttoned his jacket as if to make his weapon more accessible.

Stone got up and walked down to where Dino was sitting. "Got a minute?" he asked. Dino got up and followed him to the side of the box. "What's up?"

"Something's wrong," Stone said. "Keep looking at the theater while we talk. Agent Beam is extremely nervous and is sweating heavily. Also, he's the only agent in the box with us—we've always had at least two in the room—and he locked the door behind him and put the key into his coat pocket. That doesn't seem to me like someone who is protecting us from an attack."

"No," Dino said, "it sounds more like someone who is a threat. What do you want to do?"

Stone told him. "Let's wait until the program starts." They returned to their seats as the Los Angeles Philharmonic began to play an overture as the last stragglers got to their seats.

"Ladies and gentlemen," a voice boomed, "Miss Hattie Patrick and the Los Angeles Philharmonic Orchestra." There was loud applause as Hattie walked to the piano at the center of the stage. She sat down, the conductor raised his baton, cued the first clarinetist, who began a trill, then executed the glissando that began Gershwin's *Rhapsody in Blue*. She had performed it once before in this venue.

Stone leaned back and looked at the back of Dino's head

down the row. Dino leaned back, saw him, and nodded. They both got up and went to their respective sides of the box, then walked to the rear and approached Beam from each side. Stone smiled as he neared the man. "I have to leave the box," he said.

Beam looked alarmed and his hand slid under his jacket. Stone grabbed the man's wrist and kept him from producing the weapon while Dino drew his pistol and held it under Beam's chin. "Be very quiet," Dino whispered into his ear.

Stone separated the man's hand from his weapon and withdrew it himself. To his surprise, he found it had six inches of silencer screwed into the barrel. "Be very still," he whispered to Beam as he felt in his coat pocket for the key to the door. He found it, then spun Beam around and used the man's own handcuffs to secure his hands behind his back.

"Keep him here for a moment until I speak to the agents outside." Dino nodded. Stone unlocked the door, let himself out, and looked around. No agents in sight. Where were the four who had accompanied the tram here? He got out his cell phone and called Mike Freeman.

"Freeman."

"Mike, it's Stone. We've got a situation at the presidential box. Do you see any Secret Service?"

"Yes, there are four of them standing right here. I'm twenty yards from the box."

"Please bring them here now. And find out who is the senior agent."

"On the way."

Mike appeared with a man beside him, followed by two other men and one woman. "This is Special Agent Foster,"

Mike said. Stone shook the man's hand, held on to it and leaned in close. "Your boss, Agent Beam, is alone in the box with no other agents and behaving like a threat." Stone handed him Beam's silenced pistol. "I took this from him."

The agent looked at the pistol and his eyebrows shot up. "That is a non-standard weapon," he said.

"The NYPD chief of detectives is just inside the door. Beam is handcuffed with his own cuffs. I'll bring him out, and you should take him away quietly and leave two agents inside the box. We don't know if this is only a one-man threat." The agent nodded. Stone opened the door and motioned Dino outside. Agent Foster was speaking with his fellow agents. Two of them took away Beam, who was now in tears, and Foster and the female agent followed Stone and Dino into the box and stood by the door as they took their seats again.

Hattie was halfway through *Rhapsody in Blue*, and Stone tried to enjoy it as his eyes raked the audience for further threats.

Hattie finished her performance, then Immi Gotham took the stage and sang her way through a repertoire of Gershwin, Rodgers and Hart, Jerome Kern, and Irving Berlin. The audience was transported—and Stone would have been, too, but he was still in his most watchful mode. However, by the concert's rousing finish, no threat had appeared.

Everyone rose in a standing ovation, and Hattie, Immi, and the conductor took their bows. Stone's guests in the box had begun making their way toward the outside door and the waiting tram when the president fell in beside him.

"What was all that about with Agent Beam?" he asked.

"You'll be getting a new agent in charge of your detail," Stone replied. "It appears that the threat Beam warned us about emanated directly from Beam himself. He's in custody now, and I'm sure the detail is being reorganized as we speak."

"Nothing like this has happened during my two terms of office," Will said.

"And I expect nothing like it will happen again," Stone said.

"Do you think Beam has collaborators?"

"I'm sure that will be thoroughly investigated, but my own opinion is that he does not. His behavior was very much that of a lone wolf, and deranged people don't easily attract collaborators."

"I hope you're right," Will said.

They got into the tram, and Mike Freeman appeared and took a seat next to Stone. "We're holding Beam at our operations center," Mike said. "Other agents from the L.A. Secret Service office are on their way to take charge of him, and the rest of the detail is in place."

"The president asked if Beam had collaborators," Stone said.

"I think not," Mike replied.

The tram returned to Stone's house without incident. He and his guests went into the house for drinks and a late supper, which was laid out as a buffet in the dining room. Martin Stanton, Mark Willingham, Pete Otero, and Dick Collins, and their respective wives, joined them, though Willingham had only a drink, then excused himself.

Ed Eagle introduced Stone to Otero, and Stone found him good company. His wife, Eagle told Stone, was half Navajo. During dinner, Stone managed a seat next to Governor Dick Collins. "Yours has been quite a performance," Stone said to him.

"I've no idea what you're referring to," Collins replied with a smile.

"Nevertheless, everybody was impressed with what I'm referring to. Tomorrow night might have gotten rough after the first ballot."

"Well, I'm sure we'll have a good evening of balloting tomorrow night," Collins said, then changed the subject.

Mike Freeman found Stone alone a few minutes later. "The Secret Service has taken Mervin Beam to a hospital for a psych evaluation," he said.

"Will he be charged with anything?" Stone asked.

"Well, he didn't do anything chargeable, did he?" Mike said. "You and Dino saw to that. My guess is, he'll undergo treatment for quite some time—if he can be persuaded to commit himself. My people at our operations center said he was babbling about attacks on the Constitution and fighting for liberty, making no sense at all."

"I'd love to read the psychiatric report on him when this is all over," Stone said. "It's scary that someone who was responsible for the lives of the president and first lady could degenerate like that without someone noticing."

"You noticed," Mike said.

ANN GOT AWAY from the Oteros and joined them. "I'm going to want to hear all about what happened tonight," she said.

"I will fill you in later," Stone replied.

"What were you and Dick Collins talking about?"

"About nothing that he would admit to," Stone said.

Manolo came and got Ann and took her from the room. A minute later, she returned in the company of the female Secret Service agent who had accompanied Kate from New York on the Strategic Services jet. "Gentlemen," she said, "you met Christy Thomas on the way out here. Christy has been appointed by the director of the Secret Service to head up the presidential detail."

Everyone shook hands with her. She was about forty, Stone thought, fit-looking, fairly short brown hair, dressed in a business suit. She was a big improvement on Mervin Beam, he decided. After a little polite conversation, she stationed herself near the door, her eyes sweeping the room.

"That's a relief," Stone said to Ann.

"Yes, indeed. I've had a chance to talk with her a few times since we arrived and she's very smart. She'll make a nice change for us."

"What's on your plate for tomorrow?" Stone asked.

"Tomorrow will be surprisingly relaxed," Ann said. "Kate will be lying low, not speaking to a lot of people."

"Perhaps she would enjoy touring Centurion Studios," Stone said. "Peter would like to have us to lunch in his bungalow."

"I'll speak to her about it," Ann said, and left to do that. She returned a couple of minutes later. "She and the president would both like to come," she said. "I'd better go alert Christy Thomas. She'll have some organizing to do."

Stone took his cell phone from his pocket. "And I'd better alert Peter, and he'd better alert Leo Goldman," he said.

S tone had breakfast on the patio with Ed Eagle and
Susannah Wilde.

"Stone," Ed said, "what are you expecting to happen
with the balloting tonight at the convention?"

"Sam Meriwether, who's the expert on counting heads,
thinks Kate will get the most votes on the first ballot, and
maybe get another fifteen or twenty of the California delegates, but that won't give her the nomination. In that case, it
will go to a second ballot, and the delegates will be free. I think
they believe they can win then."

"Is there any expectation that either Willingham or Otero
will throw his delegates to Kate?"

"I haven't heard that voiced, but if either did, that would get
her the nomination. Frankly, I can't see Willingham doing
that. Maybe Otero would, though."

"Tell them not to count on Otero doing that," Eagle said.

Stone looked at him sharply. "Have you heard something?"

"I have, but I can't say what it is. I'm a member of the New Mexico delegation and we've all promised not to talk about our business with anyone else."

"Ed, do you think Otero thinks that on a second ballot he might get enough delegates for him to win the nomination?"

"I can't tell you. But remember, the convention rules state that after a second ballot of freed delegates, if no candidate has a majority, then the top two candidates will be in a runoff."

"I hadn't been thinking that far ahead," Stone said. "Anything else you can tell me?"

"No, but I can make suppositions."

"Then what do you suppose?"

"Suppose that Otero and Willingham reach an accommodation."

"What kind of accommodation?"

"Suppose they combine their delegates behind one of the candidates and the other gets chosen as his running mate?"

Stone did some quick arithmetic. "Then that candidate would have a chance of getting the nomination on the second ballot," Stone said, "if he could pick up enough of the undecideds from California and the other states."

Ed shrugged. "Let's just say that I don't think you're the only one who's thinking that way."

Stone didn't have to think that over.

Eagle changed the subject. "What are you doing with your day?" he asked.

"I'm taking Kate and the president out to Centurion Studios for a tour, and Peter's giving us all lunch."

"Peter has an excellent chef," Susannah said.

"Have you and Peter made a deal, Susannah?"

"We have. Contracts should be ready for signature in a day or two."

"Then I'll try not to run into Charlene Joiner while we're at the studio."

"I'd go armed if I were you," Susannah said.

They finished breakfast and rose to go their separate ways.

"Stone," Eagle said, "one thing I can tell you without violating a confidence: Pete Otero won't take the second spot on the ticket."

"How recently did you hear that?" Stone asked.

"About two hours ago, in a phone call."

WHEN STONE GOT back to the house, he ran into Ann, who was going into the library. "I have a meeting with Sam Meriwether," she said, "but we'll be ready to leave for Centurion at noon."

"Ann," Stone said, "would you mind if I have a word with you and Sam right now?"

"Not at all. Come in."

They went into the library, where the senior senator from Georgia was having a cup of coffee. "Good morning, Stone," he said.

Stone took a seat. "Sam, what's the latest on the delegate count?"

"As best we can tell, Kate has a hundred and eleven, Willingham eighty-nine, and Otero fifty-one," the senator said.

"Not good," Stone said.

"Well, I think that's pretty good," Meriwether said. "We won't win on the first ballot, but we probably will on the second. And if it goes to a runoff, we're a sure thing."

"And is Otero still Kate's favorite for the second spot?"

"I believe so. She dislikes and distrusts Willingham."

"Is there anyone else in the running?"

"Not that I've heard discussed in the last twenty-four hours."

"Sam, I don't have any hard information to back this up, but I have reason to think there's a deal for Willingham to throw his delegates to Otero on the first ballot, then take the number two spot on the ticket with Otero."

Meriwether shook his head. "I don't think Willingham would join the ticket of someone who's younger and, in Willingham's eyes, less qualified than he. He's got too much ego for that."

"Then let me ask you this," Stone said. "If Willingham has a choice between the second spot on the ticket and nothing, which way do you think he would jump?"

Meriwether stared at him but said nothing.

"Oh," Stone said, "one more thing: Otero told someone I trust a couple of hours ago that he would not accept the second spot on any ticket."

"Oh, shit," Meriwether said, half to himself. He picked up a phone. "I've got to call Kate. And, Ann, would you see if you can get Dick Collins over here right now?"

"Sure, Sam." She went to another phone.

KATE WAS ALREADY in the room when Governor Collins arrived.

"Kate, Dick," Meriwether said, "Stone has some information that you should hear."

Stone told them what he had just told Meriwether.

Kate looked shocked. "I really thought that Otero wanted to run on the ticket with me," she said.

"Did he ever tell you that?" Collins asked.

"No, but he asked me outright if I was going to choose a running mate before the balloting was done. I told him no, that I wouldn't trade the slot for delegates."

"Did he tell you that if you asked him, he wouldn't accept the slot on the ticket?"

"No, he didn't. It appears that Pete Otero is more ambitious than I thought."

"Do you think that Willingham would jump to Otero for the second spot on the ticket?" Collins asked.

"Stone," Meriwether said, "ask them the question you asked me."

Stone took a deep breath: "If Willingham were placed in a situation where he had to choose between the vice presidency or nothing, which way do you think he would jump?"

"Oh, shit," Collins replied.

Meriwether laughed. "Funny, that's exactly what I said."

"All right, then," Dick Collins said. "There are two things you can do, Kate."

"What are they?"

"The first is to call Willingham now and offer him the second spot on the ticket in return for his ballots."

"What's the other thing?"

"Well, if you don't want to offer it to him, you have to get enough of the undecided California delegates to go with you on the first ballot."

"How many do we have now?" Kate asked.

"Fifteen."

"And how many more undecided California delegates are there?"

"Twenty-six."

"So we need twenty-four of them, is that correct?"

"That is correct."

"All right," Kate said, "I want to tell you all something: I decided who I want for a running mate a few days ago. It's not Pete Otero. And it's *certainly* not Mark Willingham."

"Then who is it?" Meriwether asked, looking baffled.

"It's the governor of the great state of California," she replied.

Meriwether broke into a big smile. "I can live with that," he said.

"Dick," Kate said, "can you live with that?"

Collins looked at each of them separately, Kate last. "It would be my great pleasure and a great honor," he replied.

"Then you have my permission to tell any or all of your

recalcitrant delegates that if they do the right thing, the next vice president of the United States will be their governor. But tell them in the strictest confidence. We don't want Otero or Willingham getting wind of this before the voting starts."

"Right," Sam Meriwether said. "They'll wait and see how the voting goes before they make their move. Willingham will want to know how many delegates he has to pass on to Otero."

28

Harry Gregg sat outdoors at a sidewalk café on Santa Monica Beach, drinking a cup of espresso. Harry worked as a gunsmith at the Centurion Studios armory, which housed all the weapons used in Centurion productions and also rented to independents. He looked around for the person he was meeting but didn't see anyone likely. He checked his watch: five minutes before noon.

Then somebody slid into the seat opposite him. A woman. It had been a man on the phone. What was this?

"Hello, Mr. Gregg," the woman said. She was dressed in a large floppy straw hat and dark glasses, and the lower part of her face was covered by a veil as if she were afraid of getting too much sun. He couldn't even tell how old she was.

"Look over my shoulder or out to sea," she said, "not directly at me. You shouldn't want to know who I am or what I look like."

"Okay by me," Harry said, shifting in his seat to turn toward the Pacific Ocean. "I believe you're supposed to have some work for me."

"Wet work," the woman replied. "Do you know what that is?"

Harry nodded. "I've been there. Who's the lucky guy?"

"His name is Ed Eagle," she said. "Ring any bells?"

Harry had heard the name. "Lawyer?"

"Right."

"In the papers a few weeks ago, won a big murder case?"

"Right."

"Sounds like the kind of guy I'd want to hire if this went wrong."

"If you do your work well, he won't be a candidate. And you won't need a lawyer anyway."

"He's real tall, right?"

"Six feet seven. Wears good suits with cowboy boots and a Stetson."

"Right, I've seen pictures. Where do I find him?"

"He's staying at The Arrington."

Harry shook his head. "Not good—too much security. I mean, the president is staying there, you know?"

"I understand you know something about explosives."

"I know *everything* about explosives," Harry said.

"You were a navy SEAL, weren't you?"

"No, army, Special Forces. Pretty much the same thing. My specialty was booby traps."

"Oh, good," she said. "He flies an airplane called a Citation Mustang."

"I know the one—small jet."

"What would it take to blow it out of the sky?"

"You want it in tiny pieces?"

"No, it would be better if you could make it unflyable so that it would crash not long after takeoff."

"I can do that," he said. "Where is the airplane?"

"It's parked at Atlantic Aviation, on the ramp. Eagle always stops there."

"I know the place. The ramp is accessible, if you know what you're doing. How about this: they use runway 21 for takeoff and landing. Where would he be flying to?"

"Santa Fe."

"East, good. On takeoff on 21, they fly straight out over the beach and the water, then after a minute or two they turn right. How about if the airplane is disabled right at that point? It would crash into the water, breaking into a thousand pieces."

"So they could never be sure of recovering all the bits, could they?" she asked.

"Nope, that's the beauty of it."

"Do you have access to the explosives?"

"I do. And I wouldn't need more than half a pound of plastic to do the job."

"How would you set it off?"

"There are two good ways. The best is with an altimeter rigged to a detonator. How soon do I need to do this?"

"He's here for the convention and he flies back to Santa Fe

tomorrow. And he always takes off around nine A.M. He's a creature of habit."

"I can't get everything I need for the altimeter detonator by tomorrow, but I can use a cell phone."

"How do you mean?"

"I plug a cell phone into a detonator and the detonator into the plastic. Then I sit on the beach with a phone and wait for the airplane to take off. All I have to do is make a call and, poof! your problem, whatever it is, is solved."

"Ideal," she said.

"This one is going to cost you five-zero grand."

"That's very steep," she said.

"I'm sure you can find somebody cheaper," Harry said and made to get up.

"Sit down."

He sat.

She pushed a thick envelope into his hand. "There's twenty-five thousand in there," she said, "and you'll get the other twenty-five right here, tomorrow at noon, if you've been successful."

"And if I'm not?"

"Then you will still be here at noon and bring me twenty back. The five is for your trouble."

Harry took the envelope and put it into his coat pocket. "I'll count it later," he said. "What's the tail number of the airplane?"

She told him. "They always park it on the ramp, west of the hangars. There'll be a line of airplanes parked there."

"I know the place."

"Stay here and have some lunch," she said. "Then get to work." She got up and left.

Harry watched her back as she walked away from the café. "Nice ass," he said aloud to himself.

S tone and Ann rode in the presidential limousine with the president and first lady. The gate guard at Centurion Studios was ready for them and waved the three-car motorcade through the big front gates. A few yards behind them were more cars, carrying Secret Service agents, the president's secretary, and a physician—and a young naval officer carrying a valise called "the Football," which contained the codes for initiating a nuclear attack. The limousine glided to a halt in front of the production company's bungalow, the passengers got out, then all the vehicles pulled into the parking lot across the street and waited.

Peter and Ben greeted them at the door as Hattie and Tessa waited inside. The two partners took the group through the various rooms—Hattie's studio, with its Steinway concert grand piano, the editing suite, and the offices, where they shook hands with Billy and Betsy Burnett. Finally, they emerged onto a recently constructed rear deck that offered a sweeping view of the sprawling studio lot. A large round table was set for lunch, and waiters hovered nearby.

Leo Goldman Jr. showed up, greeted everyone, and joined them for lunch.

Before Stone could begin to eat, his cell phone went off. He checked the caller ID: Dick Collins. Stone excused himself, went inside, and answered the phone.

"Stone, it's Dick Collins."

"Good morning, Governor—or, rather, good afternoon."

"I didn't want to call Kate directly, but you can tell her that, after many phone calls this morning, Sam Meriwether and I now put her delegate count at a hundred and thirty-five."

"Exactly what's needed to nominate?"

"Exactly."

"No margin for error, then."

"We'll be working the rest of the day to move undecideds in other delegations to Kate's side and we hope to come up with as many as half a dozen more."

"Will you keep me posted on that?" Stone asked.

"Certainly."

"It's going to be an exciting evening," Stone said.

"I hope not too exciting," Collins said, then hung up.

Stone went back to the table and leaned between the president and first lady. "Dick Collins says you have a hundred and thirty-five delegates, and he and Sam will be working all day on rounding up, maybe, another half dozen."

"Thank you, Stone," Kate said. "Now, let's try to enjoy our lunch."

Stone took his seat next to Leo Goldman, who was sitting next to Kate.

"How's the vote count going?" Leo asked him quietly.

"Close," Stone said.

"Close good or close bad?"

"Ask me late tonight."

Leo nodded and went back to talking movies with Kate and Will.

After lunch, a tram waited, led and followed by Secret Service vehicles. Everyone boarded, and they set off on the tour. Leo Goldman gave a running account of the history of Centurion and showed them the famous New York City street standing set, which had been featured in dozens of movies, then they visited the costume department and were admitted to the studio's largest sound stage, where three different sets had been constructed and dressed, among them a Fifth Avenue apartment.

"I could move right into this place," Kate said. "It's bigger than our apartment at the Carlyle." Leo opened the doors to the master suite dressing room, which was stuffed with expensive women's clothing, with shelves of handbags and shoes. "I don't know who this woman is," Kate said, "but she has a *much* better wardrobe than I."

They visited the Centurion armory, where Kate and Will

got to fire a few rounds from a Winchester Model 73, assisted by the armory gunsmith, Harry Gregg. They posed for a picture with him, and Kate shook his hand warmly. "I'm told you served with Special Forces in Afghanistan and I want to thank you for your service," she said. Harry blushed. Then they went on to the big garage where the studio's collection of vintage vehicles was kept, along with a stock of contemporary cars and trucks.

They finished up at the studio commissary, where dessert and coffee were waiting for the party. As they entered, they got a standing ovation from the assorted producers, directors, writers, technicians, and actors who were lunching there, many of them familiar faces to any moviegoer.

After dessert and coffee and much handshaking, they got back onto the tram and toured the back lot, with its lake and its western town and small-town-square sets.

Stone's cell phone rang again. It was Ed Eagle.

"We've just come out of a caucus, Stone, and something's going on. Pete Otero wasn't there, and it's the first caucus he's missed."

"Do you know where he is?" Stone asked.

"No, and he's always been very visible to his delegates."

"Ed, do you think any of your delegates might break for Kate on the first ballot?"

"I doubt it. Pete won our primary, and it might be politically dangerous for anyone to cross him at the convention. He's still got two more years in his second term, and he knows how to reward his friends and punish his enemies."

"Does that include you?"

"He and I are pretty good friends. As much as I like Kate and Will, I won't break from Pete on the first ballot."

"What do you think Otero might do if he learned, before his delegation is called on to vote, that Kate was looking the likely winner?"

"I'm not sure," Ed said.

"Is he politically astute enough to get behind her if it looks like he's losing?"

"He's certainly politically astute," Ed said, "but I'm not sure what it would take to convince him that he can't win. I mean, Kate's not likely to have all the votes she needs when the voting gets down to the Ns, is she?"

"We think she's likely to have enough without New Mexico and Virginia," Stone said.

"I'm going to have to do some arithmetic," Ed said, "then see how the voting is going before New Mexico is called on. Are you going to be on the floor?"

"No, I'll be in the skybox, but my cell works there."

"I'll call you if I have news."

"Thanks, Ed, I'd appreciate that." Stone hung up and got back onto the tram with the others.

"What's going on?" Ann asked.

"Looks like Kate is right on the edge," he said.

"Oh, God, I don't know if I can take the balloting," Ann said.

"Will you be in the skybox with me?"

"Sure. I can't do anything back at the hotel."

"You'll be only a phone call away from Kate."

"I think that she and the president may want to be alone

141

anyway. If she wins the nomination, they won't have much time together again until after the election."

"Just tell her you'll be with me. She can always reach you if she needs to."

"All right, I'll do that."

30

*L*ate in the day, Billy Burnett was returning from the set to the offices in his golf cart when he passed a construction site for a new sound stage. The construction crew worked from seven A.M. to three P.M., so the site was deserted. Except it wasn't.

Billy stopped his cart and watched as a familiar figure strode across the site. The young man stopped, looked around, and didn't see Billy. It was Harry Gregg, the gunsmith at the Centurion armory whom Billy had hired and trained the year before, and there was something furtive about his actions.

Sure that he was alone, Harry began doing something to the door lock on the construction shed in which hand tools and explosives were stored. Billy glanced at his watch, then waited patiently until Harry emerged from the shed. He had been there for a little less than two minutes and he was carrying something in a brown paper bag. He watched as Harry got into a golf cart and drove back to the armory.

Billy drove back to his office, lost in thought. He'd have a word with Harry tomorrow. The young man always came in early to get a head start on his work.

HARRY TOOK HIS paper bag into the now-deserted armory and went to his workroom. He weighed the bag: six and a half ounces. Plenty. He molded the malleable plastic explosive into the desired shape, then unwrapped a throwaway cell phone he had bought at his neighborhood supermarket and plugged it in for charging. The battery was already eighty percent charged, so he didn't have to wait long. He cut a piece of wire, stripped the ends of their insulation, secured one end to a detonator he had taken from the construction shack, and pressed the detonator into the soft explosive, then he used duct tape to fix the cell phone to the explosive, satisfied that it had a sufficient charge. He did not fix the detonator wire to the phone—not yet. Safety first, he told himself.

Harry put the completed bomb and some tools and duct tape into his tin lunchbox, then went home. As he walked into his apartment, his phone was ringing and he picked it up.

"This is your client," a woman's voice said. "The gentleman you seek will depart at nine A.M. the day after tomorrow, not tomorrow. All other arrangements are the same. Do you understand?"

"Yes," he said, and she hung up.

———

STONE AND ANN arrived at the Staples Center with the Bacchettis in an Arrington SUV and, after the usual security procedures, took the elevator up to Stone's skybox.

The bartender brought them drinks, and Stone picked up a pair of binoculars and stood at the big window, panning around the convention floor. He found the New Mexico delegation—only five delegates, but with various spouses and hangers-on seated with them they came to fifteen or twenty, including Ed Eagle, who stood head and shoulders above the rest. Pete Otero was not in sight.

Stone kept panning until he found the Virginia delegation— bigger than that of New Mexico, with thirteen delegates. Senator Mark Willingham was not among them.

He did the same for the huge California delegation. With its fifty-five delegates and their hangers-on it came to more than a hundred people. Governor Dick Collins stood in the midst of them, shaking hands and buttonholing delegates, whispering intently into an ear here and there.

Stone called Ed Eagle, who answered immediately. "Hi there, I've got binoculars on you."

Ed turned and looked up at the skybox and waved.

"Where's your governor?"

"I don't know—not here, though."

"Funny, Willingham isn't with his delegation, either."

"Train your binoculars to the right, under the first balcony. There's a bar."

Stone panned right. "Got it." Ah, there were the missing

pols, in earnest conversation. "Otero has Willingham by a lapel. I'll bet he doesn't like that, but he's nodding, so they must be in agreement. Powwow is breaking up now. Your governor will be with you in a moment."

"I'd better go," Eagle said and hung up.

Stone watched Otero work his way across the floor, shaking hands, smiling, slapping a back here and there, pecking women on the cheek. Then he found Willingham, rigid in his pin-striped suit, greeting men—only men. He apparently didn't have much use for women, and it didn't take him long to rejoin his delegation.

"Well," Stone said to Dino, who stood beside him, "all the players are where they're supposed to be."

The convention was being hammered to order by the chairman, who was shouting at the delegates to take their seats.

Stone took a seat next to Ann, found a remote control, and turned on the TV sets to get the play-by-play.

BACK IN THE library of The Arrington's presidential cottage, Will and Kate Lee sat, having dinner off trays. Kate put her fork down. "I don't think I can eat."

"Funny, I'm starved," Will said, shoving a slab of steak into his mouth and sipping from a glass of Cabernet.

"Well," Kate said, "that's the difference between an office seeker and an officeholder—and a lame duck at that."

———

CHRIS MATTHEWS WAS holding forth on the balloting. "Kate Lee has taken an early lead," he said. "Arizona, whose delegates Martin Stanton won in the primary, went solidly for her, but Alabama and Alaska went for Willingham. California has put the first lady ahead—she got forty-two of her fifty-five delegates. And Otero got the rest."

STONE SAT UP. "Thirteen went to Otero? Dick wasn't able to swing them all."

"That could hurt us later in the balloting," Ann said, chewing her lip and taking a swig of her martini. "God, I hate this part."

S tone looked over Ann's shoulder at the running totals she was keeping on a legal pad. "Kate can't be that far off Sam's projection," he said.

"Hang on, here comes Illinois." Illinois's twenty delegates were voted for Kate.

"That's better," Stone said, relieved.

"Yes, but we're only twelve votes ahead. And we've got some Willingham and Otero states coming."

Kansas cast six votes for Otero and Missouri ten for Willingham.

"Why is Otero so far behind?" Stone asked.

"Texas," Ann replied. "Second-largest delegate count. When we get to the Ts, Texas will bring Otero up to fiftyish."

"How long before we get to the Ns?" Stone asked.

"Soon."

Stone called Ed Eagle.

"Yes, Stone?"

"Ed, how would you like to elect the next president of the United States?"

"Personally?"

"Personally."

"How do I do that?"

"Take Otero aside and tell him that Kate is going to win it on the first ballot."

"Are you sure?"

"Very nearly," Stone lied. "Do it now, Ed, and it will be over. She won't need him or Willingham. Tell Otero if he throws his delegates to Kate, he'll be in the good graces of the next president. Or if he sticks it out with Willingham, he'll be number one on Kate's shit list. And tell him anything else you can think of."

"I'll call you back," Eagle said.

Stone picked up the binoculars and trained them on the New Mexico delegation. Eagle had taken Otero into an aisle, a few steps away from the others. Ed was looking down at Otero and Otero was looking at the floor with an ear cocked toward Ed. Otero was shaking his head vehemently.

"Oh, shit," Stone said, lowering the binoculars. "Where are we in the ballot count?"

"Projecting one thirty-one," Ann said. "This is not good, Stone. Somebody is making a lot of promises to delegates who committed to Kate."

Stone raised the binoculars again. Otero and Eagle were gone. He swept the New Mexico delegation; they were not there. Where the hell were they? New Mexico would be called on in a minute or two. Then he spotted them: they were striding toward the Virginia delegation, and Willingham had just seen them coming. "Something's going on," Stone said, half to himself.

"What? What's going on?" Ann asked.

"Powwow at the Virginia delegation. Ed and Otero are over there. Ed is doing all the talking."

KATE LOOKED OVER Will's shoulder at the chicken-scratching on his pad. "What does all that mean?" she asked.

"I'm a little confused," Will said. "We seem to be three or four votes behind where we should be at this point. Where the hell is Sam Meriwether?"

"With the Georgia delegation," Kate replied.

"See if you can get him on the phone."

Kate called the number and put the phone on speaker.

"Kate?"

"Sam, Will's worried about the delegate count."

"He should damn well be worried," Sam replied. "By my projections, we'll be three votes short of the nomination. And if that happens, then Otero and Willingham will join forces on the second ballot and take the nomination. Oh, and Otero is over at the Virginia delegation right now with Willingham. They're cooking up something."

"Sam," Will said, "drop everything and get over to Virginia. See if you can break up whatever they're thinking about."

"I'll call you back," Meriwether said.

"Will, I'm sorry I ever did this," Kate said, resting her forehead on his shoulder.

"You just hang on, sweetheart, it's not over yet."

"I just have this awful feeling in the pit of my stomach."

"Have a bourbon and Alka-Seltzer that always works for me."

"NEW MEXICO!" the chairman was shouting.

Stone watched as a New Mexican he didn't know stood up and took the microphone. Otero was nowhere in sight.

"Mr. Chairman," the man shouted, "I am the deputy chairman of the New Mexico delegation. I request a poll of the delegation!"

The audience roared with laughter. There were only five delegates and they were sitting next to one another.

"That was funny," Stone said.

"They're buying time," Ann said. "I don't like this."

The chairman began calling the names of the New Mexico delegation. When he got to Ed Eagle, there was no response.

Stone checked the Virginia delegation again. Willingham was there but Otero and Eagle were not.

"New Mexico, do you wish to cast only four votes?"

"One moment, Mr. Chairman," the deputy delegation leader said, looking desperately around the floor.

Then Pete Otero strode up and took the microphone away from the man. Ed Eagle was standing beside him. "Mr.

Chairman, I am Pete Otero, governor of the great state of New Mexico!" he shouted.

The chairman shouted back, "I thought you looked familiar!"

The audience roared with laughter again.

"Mr. Chairman," Otero said again, "at this time I wish to withdraw from the race for the presidential nomination of the Democratic Party."

There was a mixed audience roar, cheers and *Nooo*s.

"Mr. Chairman," Otero shouted, "the New Mexico delegation casts all its votes, and I request all delegates pledged to me to vote for the next president of the United States, Katharine Lee!"

The audience went crazy. The chairman put up with it for a couple of minutes, then began hammering the podium with his gavel. Then, as the roar subsided, another voice was heard.

"Mr. Chairman, I am Senator Mark Willingham of Virginia and I wish to be recognized."

"This is irregular, Senator," the chairman said, "but you are recognized."

"Mr. Chairman," Willingham shouted, "I wish to withdraw at this time from consideration for the Democratic nomination for president. And, further, I release all delegates pledged to me and urge them to cast their votes for the next president of the United States, Katharine Lee of Georgia!"

Pandemonium reigned. The chairman hammered for order without effect. Stone looked over at the New Mexico delegation and saw Pete Otero standing on a chair, keeping his balance by hanging on to Ed Eagle's shoulder. "Mr. Chairman!" he was yelling. "Mr. Chairman!"

Finally regaining some order, the chairman pointed at Otero. "The chair recognizes the governor of the great state of New Mexico, Pete Otero!"

"Mr. Chairman," Otero yelled, "I move that the convention nominate by acclamation as its nominee for president, Katharine Lee of Georgia!"

A huge affirmative roar from the audience.

The chairman hammered again. "The chair recognizes Senator Mark Willingham of the great state of Virginia!"

Willingham grabbed a microphone and yelled, "Mr. Chairman, I second Governor Otero's motion!"

"All in favor, holler!" the chairman shouted.

And the crowd hollered for a full seven minutes.

S tone and Ann were hugging each other and laughing, and Dino was pounding him on the back. Viv was pointing at the turmoil on the convention floor and laughing.

Ann called Kate, but her line was busy. "We'll never be able to get through to Kate," she said. Then Ann's phone rang.

"Hello?"

"It's Kate. Turn off the TV."

Stone turned it off and Ann pressed the speaker button.

"Congratulations, Kate!"

"You mean what I just saw really happened?"

"It certainly did."

Will's voice came on the line. "Stone, what was Ed Eagle doing with Otero and Willingham?"

"I'm looking forward to asking him that, Mr. President,"

Stone said, "but whatever he was doing, it seems to have worked."

"If you see Eagle, please have him call me."

"Yes, sir!"

"Ann, Stone," Kate said, "thanks for your congratulations, but you'll have to excuse me, I think I should take some incoming calls!"

"Yes, ma'am!" Ann ended the connection. "May I have another drink, please?"

Stone waved at a waiter. "Open some champagne," he said. Then someone was hammering on the skybox door. Stone opened it, and Ed Eagle, Susannah Wilde, and Mike Freeman spilled into the room. The hall outside was crammed with people.

Stone got the door shut. "Come on in, we're starting on the champagne," he said. A waiter came with flutes and poured the wine. Stone raised his glass. "To Ed Eagle and whatever he said to Otero and Willingham." They drank. "Ed, what did you say to Otero and Willingham?"

"Exactly what you told me to say," Ed replied. "I may have been a little more emphatic, though."

"We were going crazy up here watching you with binoculars."

"Otero got it immediately," Eagle said, "but he didn't want to get it. Then he grabbed me and dragged me over to the Virginia delegation and got ahold of Willingham. The senator was adamant—tried to talk Pete out of it, but Pete didn't budge. Finally, Willingham did the arithmetic, swore a few times, and said, 'Okay.' The rest you heard on TV."

"We had a hell of a time getting off the floor," Mike said. "The aisles were solid with delegates, a lot of them getting drunk in a hurry. Has anybody talked with Kate?"

"She just hung up to start taking congratulatory calls," Stone said. "Ed, the president asked that you call him." He produced his cell phone, pressed the button, and handed the phone to Eagle.

"Hello, Mr. President? Yes, sir." He walked across the room and kept talking into the phone. A couple of minutes later he hung up and rejoined the others.

Stone pointed at the television set. "You're on TV, Ed," he said, switching on the sound. Chris Matthews was talking.

"We still don't know exactly what happened," he was saying, "but that tall guy standing next to Otero had something to do with it. His name is Ed Eagle. He's a big-time trial lawyer from Santa Fe, and he's a New Mexico delegate. He and Otero went over to the Virginia delegation—Wait a minute, we have tape on that—there, Eagle and Otero arguing with Senator Mark Willingham of Virginia, and whatever they're saying, the senator isn't buying it. Now he buys it: he's nodding at Otero, then Otero and Eagle go back to the New Mexico seats, where the delegation is being polled, all five of them, much to the amusement of the crowd. Then Otero grabs the microphone, and you know the rest."

Ed laughed. "I didn't know I was on TV," he said. "I'll catch hell about that when I get back to Santa Fe."

"I guarantee you," Stone said, "every TV reporter on the floor is looking for you right now."

"Then I'm staying here," Ed said. "I'll sleep here if I have to."

"What did the president have to say to you?" Stone asked.

"The same thing you said to me when I got here," Ed replied. "I talked to Kate, too. She's pretty excited."

"I'll bet she is."

"Oh, when I took Otero aside and started in on him and told him what you said about the delegate count, the first thing Pete said was, 'Who the hell is Stone Barrington, and why should I believe him?' I told him you were the smartest guy in the hall and had the only accurate delegate count, and that Sam Meriwether was feeding it to you. Was I lying?"

"Not exactly, Ed, but when I talked to Sam, he was still pretty worried about how the count was going."

"Then you were bluffing?"

"Let's just say I was a little optimistic."

"Well, it worked. That's poker—if you can't tell who's bluffing, you're being bluffed!"

"Well, I'm glad I didn't have to do it face-to-face with Otero and Willingham," Stone said. "They would probably have called me on it!"

Ann settled into a sofa. "Turn the TV back on. I'm not leaving here until all those people down there go home!"

S tone and Ann didn't get home until well after mid-
night, and they slept until after eight o'clock, late for
them. Ann had turned her phone off the night before,
and when she checked her voice mail there was a message from Kate, left only minutes before.

"It's chaotic over here," Kate said. "I hope it's okay if Will
and I come over there for breakfast because we're on our way!"

"Oh, shit," Ann said, running for the shower. "Kate and
Will are probably downstairs demanding breakfast!"

Stone picked up the phone and ascertained that this was
true. "Give them whatever they want," Stone said. "We'll be
down in fifteen minutes."

They made it in that time to find the Lees digging into
omelets on the patio by the pool. They joined them.

"You look very well rested," Kate said.

"Thank you," Stone replied, "so do you."

"I can't believe how well I slept," Kate said.

Stone ordered breakfast for him and Ann, then looked up to see Sam Meriwether approaching; he waved him to a chair, and Sam ordered breakfast. "They said at your place that you were over here," he said to Kate and Will.

"As you see us," Will replied.

Sam shook his head. "I still don't know what happened last night. Dick Collins and I ran the numbers over and over, and as best we could figure, we were going to be three delegates short at the end of the voting—Dick said four. Then if we had gone to a second ballot, Otero and Willingham could have taken the nomination. I don't understand it. Why did they fold when they did?"

"I can enlighten you," Will said. "I have it from the horse's mouth—that is, Ed Eagle's. It went like this: Stone, here, called Ed on the floor and told him to tell Otero that we had the votes to win on the first ballot. Otero didn't believe it at first, but Ed brought him around, then they went over to Virginia and sandbagged Mark Willingham. That was it: Otero went back to his delegation and conceded, then Willingham folded, too."

"Wait a minute," Sam said. "You're telling me we won the nomination on a *bluff*?"

"That's what I'm telling you," Will said. "And I don't think Stone will deny it."

"Stone?" Sam said incredulously. "Is that what happened?"

Stone shrugged. "Ann ran the numbers, and somebody had to do something. I'm sorry we didn't have time to check with you or Kate, Sam, but we had to move New Mexico off the

159

dime before the chairman called on them to vote, otherwise it would have been over."

"Well," Kate said, "we couldn't have that, could we?"

"I swear to God," Sam said, "it would never have occurred to me to bluff."

"That's because you're such a nice, honest, straightforward man, Sam," Kate said, "whereas Stone . . ."

"Stone," Ann said, "you're blushing."

"My true character has been revealed," Stone said.

"And a truer character never lived," Kate said. "What would you like in the new administration, Stone? Attorney general? Ambassador to the Court of Saint James's? Appointment to the first vacancy at the Supreme Court? Name it!" Everybody was laughing now.

"Maybe ambassador to Tonga," Stone said, "or anyplace with good beaches, golf courses, and little work to do."

"I'll see what I can do," Kate said.

KATE AND WILL finished their breakfast. "Do you mind if we hang out here for a while, Stone?" Will asked. "Our phones are jammed with calls from people who want something from Kate."

"Please stay as long as you like, indoors or out," Stone replied.

Manolo approached. "Mr. Stone," he said, "there are people calling the house for you." He handed Stone a sheet of paper with a dozen names of TV and print reporters. "They all want to interview you."

Stone ran through the list. "Oh, God," he said.

"Word is getting around about last night, Stone," Will said.

"What is your advice, Will? Should I talk to these people?"

"My advice is to remain an enigma for as long as you can. You're going to read and hear a great many reports in the various media concerning the events of last night, some of them less favorable than others. Let the dust settle for a while, then, at some later date of your own choosing, decide who, if anybody, you want to confide in."

"That's good advice, Will."

"If you like," Ann said, "you can refer all requests for interviews to me and I'll tell them all, 'No comment.'"

"Done," Stone replied.

34

Late in the afternoon, Billy Burnett could no longer contain his curiosity. He drove his cart over to the armory and walked in. Jake, who ran the place, was at his bench working on a disassembled AR-15. "Hey, Jake."

"Hey, Billy."

"How's it going?" Billy was looking around but couldn't see Harry Gregg anywhere.

"It's going good. You did a good job breaking in Harry. I thank you for it. It's taken a load off, you know?"

"Where is Harry?" Billy asked.

"He asked for a couple days off," Jake said. "He bought a little house in Venice, and he's doing some work on it."

"Where in Venice?"

"On the beach—dunno where."

"How the hell can Harry afford a place on Venice Beach?" Billy asked.

"Not my business," Jake said. "Harry'll be back the day after tomorrow. You want something with him?"

"No, I just wondered why he wasn't here."

"Anything else I can do for you?"

"Nope. See you around, Jake." Billy got into his cart and drove slowly back to the office. He found this news troubling. Harry was less than a year out of the army, and he was making sixty grand a year at the armory. How could a recent veteran earn enough money to buy on Venice Beach? Something occurred to him: Harry's skills were in the use and repair of firearms and in making explosive devices go boom. Who would pay a lot of money for those skills? Well, that was obvious: people who wanted other people shot or blown up. And Harry, only the day before, had made some sort of a withdrawal from a shed used to house explosives.

Billy, back when he was still Teddy Fay, had killed people, but he had never done it for money, and he frowned on the practice. Maybe he should have a chat with Harry. Or, on the other hand, maybe he should just mind his own business. He decided to do that.

STONE HAD SPENT the morning by the pool reading the papers, and it got to be lunchtime. Ed Eagle came over from the house, and they ordered club sandwiches and beers.

"I've been getting a lot of phone calls from the media," Ed said.

"So have I," Stone replied. "Will Lee's advice was to lie low, and that's what I'm doing."

"Then I'll do the same," Ed said. "Anyway, we're getting out of here first thing tomorrow morning, and they won't chase me to Santa Fe."

"I wouldn't count on that," Stone said.

"I got an odd piece of news this morning," Eagle said. "I was speaking with a client of mine who has a problem and needs my advice. He's got a house for sale in Bel-Air, and he got an offer from somebody named Grosvenor."

"Funny," Stone said, "I know somebody named Charles Grosvenor who's looking for a Bel-Air house."

Eagle stared at him. "Why didn't you mention that?"

Stone frowned. "Why would I do that? The guy's a Brit who's moving to L.A. My office asked me to meet with him, and I introduced him to the managing partner of our L.A. office at a lunch at the Bel-Air."

"Stone," Eagle said, "Charles Grosvenor is Barbara's most recent husband. They live in San Francisco."

"Can't be the same guy," Stone said. "I met his wife and she doesn't look anything like Barbara."

"Barbara is very good at not looking anything like Barbara," Eagle said. "Describe her."

"Maybe early forties, slim, busty, straight gray hair to her shoulders." Stone remembered something else. "Uh-oh, American."

"Where did you last see her?"

"At the Bel-Air lunch a couple of days ago."

"Barbara likes the Bel-Air," Eagle said. "She murdered somebody there once. Thinking it was me, she put a bullet in the man's head as he slept."

"That's right, she did, didn't she? She doesn't know you're in town, does she?"

"If she watches TV or reads the papers, she knows," Eagle said. "You and I are all over them. In any case, she'd know I'd be at the convention—I never miss one."

"Ed, maybe you should talk to Mike Freeman about a little personal security while you're in town."

Eagle didn't seem to hear him. "Last time, she hired somebody—a stunt man from out at Centurion. He missed, so she killed *him*." He seemed to remember that Stone had said something. "I'm sorry, did you say something about personal security?"

"I'd be glad to talk to Mike Freeman for you."

"Let's think ahead," Eagle said. "Security at The Arrington is pretty good."

"Better than good," Stone pointed out, "especially while the president is here."

"Right. And we'll be in your skybox for Kate's speech tonight, so I should be okay there."

"Right."

"And we're out of here tomorrow morning."

"If you're comfortable, then I'll try not to worry about you."

"I'm never going to feel completely comfortable, knowing that Barbara and I are in the same town at the same time," Eagle said, "but I can't let myself get paranoid about it."

"Don't go armed tonight," Stone said. "You'd never make it into the hall."

"Don't mention this to Susannah," Eagle said. "She'd find Barbara and kill her."

"You don't need that," Stone said.

"I do, but you're right, I don't," Eagle replied.

S tone and his guests, the Bacchettis, the Eagles, and Ann
Keaton, were settled in the skybox while the conventioneers took their seats. Tonight's program was short.

Promptly at six o'clock the lights dimmed, music
swelled, and an enormous screen on the stage came to life.
For the next thirty minutes, the audience followed Will Lee
from his boyhood in Delano, Georgia, through university and
law school, through his tenure as a legislative assistant and
later chief of staff to the legendary senator from Georgia, Ben-
jamin Carr, and as counsel to the Senate Select Committee on
Intelligence. There was a brief snip of Will questioning Katharine Rule, a CIA analyst, who was testifying on an agency
budget request, their first meeting. The film then followed
Kate's rise at the Agency to deputy director for intelligence,
her marriage to Will, and finally to the passage of an act of

Congress that allowed him to appoint her director of Central Intelligence. Brief attention was given to some of the crises where she was a principal adviser to the president, then to their travels around the world together, when she acted as both adviser and first lady. Then, as the film faded to black and the room to darkness, a voice proclaimed, "Ladies and gentlemen, the president of the United States." As Will Lee strode from the wings and took the podium to wild applause from the audience, the armored glass curtain rose from the floor.

He finally got them quieted. "Fellow delegates, honored guests, ladies and gentlemen," he began, "I am rapidly running out of occasions where I can address an event this large . . . and this friendly . . . so I have a great deal of gratitude to spread around, and that is best done to a captive audience. Don't try to make a break for it, the doors are closed and guarded." Big laugh.

"Most of the people who made it possible for me to be elected to this job, then be reelected, are in this room. I thank you, one and all, for every word of advice you gave, every favor you extended, every dollar you contributed, and every push you gave me toward the presidency. I also want to thank many of my opponents for the office who, with their soaring oratory and loose grip on the facts, made me look better than I had a right to. I could never have done it without their help." Big laugh. "Far too many of my best friends were unable to be here tonight, summoned to a higher calling. First among them is Senator Ben Carr, that master legislator and brilliant senator at whose knee I learned nearly enough to get me through my

Senate years and to the White House. His like will not be heard again on the Senate floor, and I still miss him.

"Now, before I yield the podium, I have three duties to perform: the first is to reiterate a promise I made to the nation not very long ago: I shall support the nominee of my party for the office of president of the United States!" The crowd roared with laughter. When he had calmed them he continued: "My second duty is to place in nomination the name of the man who will be the running mate for our candidate and who will be the next vice president of the United States. He has distinguished himself as a fine state senator, as a brilliant mayor of a major American city, and as an outstandingly effective governor of our most populous state, and he is now ready to take the national stage and occupy the second-highest office in the land. It is my great honor and even greater pleasure to place in nomination for the Democratic candidate for vice president of the United States, the name of the governor of the great state of California, Richard Collins!" Huge roar. Will waited for it to subside, then cupped a hand behind his ear. "Do I hear a second?"

"Second!" the huge crowd shouted.

Will picked up the gavel and hammered it once. "The motion is adopted by acclamation!"

Demonstrations now took place in the aisles, and the band played. Eventually, order was restored.

"I have one further duty," Will said, "before I slink into the ignominy of lame-duckhood. I must say that this duty gives me the greatest pleasure of my life—so far. It is my great honor to introduce to you a person who has already, in the many years of her public service, done more for her country than have most presidents, and done it quietly, behind the scenes in ways often brilliant, but necessarily concealed, that the public cannot know about for decades to come, who has always put her country first in her life and work, and who now seeks to come into the bright light of an election and seek the highest office in the land—one that she richly deserves.

"My fellow Americans," Will shouted, "the next president of the United States, Katharine Lee!"

KATE WALKED BRISKLY from the wings, clad in a red suit, setting off her blond hair. She stood at one side of the podium, then the other, waving, pointing at people she knew and those she didn't, then she returned and stood quietly at the podium until the last of the applause died. She reached forward, pressed a button on the podium, and the thick glass security screen descended into the floor. Kate leaned into the microphone and said, "I never want anything between you and me but air." And the crowd went crazy again.

Finally, after she had quiet, Kate began to speak, without notes or teleprompter, which had disappeared with the glass screen. "I stand before you a proud but chastened woman, for today I have learned what every nominee for the presidency before me has felt—that accepting the Democratic nomination for the presidency is not something that can be taken lightly. It is a heavy responsibility, and I accept it. I accept your nomination!"

Much cheering.

"Next week, we begin this campaign in earnest, and when it is over, Governor Richard Collins and I will have visited every state and told their citizens what we plan to do in office, so I will not give you that long list now. Suffice it to say that we will continue the policies of my brilliant predecessor!"

Laughter.

"We will meet you at the center, where the work gets done!" This had been Will Lee's campaign slogan. "We will use the Internet and social media to state our proposals in detail, since personal appearances are all too brief. I want every American to know what we stand for and what we won't stand for!"

The crowd went wild yet again. When the applause petered out, Kate went on.

"But there is something I want every American to hear now," she said. "The most important question any candidate is asked: 'Why do you want to be president?' I want to be president because my upbringing, my education in school, at university and law school, my work as an intelligence officer and my leadership as the director of Central Intelligence, my time in the White House, and my very close relationship with my president and my contributions to his policy decisions— all these have given me a unique set of qualifications, and I want to put those to work, as I have always done, in the service of my country. I want to heal old wounds and break new ground. I want to conduct the necessary and constant rebuilding of our nation while forging ahead in new domestic and foreign policy. And if elected, I want to do what Will Lee has done—leave my successor with a better country than when I started."

Much applause.

"I ask of my countrymen more than their votes for me, I ask them to give me a Congress that is committed to our ideals as a nation and that will be ready to work hard every day for our people. If my countrymen will do that, then Dick Collins and I, with the support of a hardworking Congress, will give them an even better America!"

Kate stepped back from the microphone and waved to Dick Collins, who was in the wings, to come onstage. They embraced, then clasped hands and waved as the band began to play and the crowd cheered themselves to hoarseness.

UP IN STONE'S skybox he and his guests poured champagne, toasted the new nominees, then sat down to dinner while the crowd below began to drift toward the exits.

In the predawn hours of the morning of the following day, Harry Gregg left his pickup truck in a parking lot adjacent to Santa Monica Airport and made the short hike down the road past Atlantic Aviation. He saw no one, and no one saw him.

He found a place where the chain-link fence surrounding the airport was concealed from the road by tall bushes, and scrambled between them to reach the fence. He took a set of short-handled bolt cutters from his backpack and made a three-foot horizontal cut of the fence near where the chain link disappeared into the ground, then another vertical cut alongside a fence pole. He peeled back the fence and let himself in, then pressed the chain link back into place. He stood quietly for a couple of minutes, listening for vehicles or footsteps. The airport was closed overnight, so there was no aircraft noise. Satisfied that he was alone, he walked over to the taxiway and began to move along the line of airplanes parked there. He saw two Citation Mustangs before he came to the one with the correct tail number.

Once again, he stopped and listened. Nothing. He knelt beside the nosewheel, took a small but very powerful lithium-powered flashlight from his pocket, and carefully examined the well into which the nosewheel would be retracted during flight. Once again, he stopped, looked around, and listened. Still nothing to disturb him.

He removed the explosive device he had built and, for the first time, connected the wire from the detonator to the cell phone that would activate it. He opened the clamshell phone and taped the top flap to the bomb, then he stuffed the bomb all the way up into the wheel well and taped it to the shaft of the nosewheel. He examined the installation carefully, then, satisfied that all was well, he switched on the bomb's cell phone.

SEVERAL MILES AWAY, in a bar no more than a block from Harry's Venice Beach house, a screenwriter named Aaron Zell sat on a stool and rattled the ice in his empty glass. "One more, Phil," he said.

"Coming up," the bartender replied. He filled a clean glass with ice, then filled it with the twelve-year-old scotch that his customer had been drinking since three A.M. and set it in front of him. "What're you doing here alone tonight?" Phil asked. "Where's your girl?"

"We had a fight," Zell said. "I don't even know what about."

"I've had fights like that with women," Phil said, fulfilling his role as sympathetic bartender. "You never know what'll set 'em off."

"Too fucking right," Zell replied. He took his cell phone from his pocket and began to dial a number.

"So you're going to fix things by waking her up in the middle of the night?" Phil asked.

"She never sleeps after a fight," Zell said. "We once made a pact that we'd never go to sleep angry with each other." The numbers on the cell phone were a little blurred, given how much he had drunk, and he got the number wrong. "Call failed," the on-screen message said.

"Shit, dialed it wrong," Zell said. He tried picking out the number again, and put the phone to his ear. This time, the phone rang once, stopped. "Now what?" he said.

HARRY GREGG STUCK his head as far up into the Mustang's wheel well as he could, switched on his flashlight, and made a final inspection of his bomb. Then he heard something he had not expected. The cell phone that he had just taped to the explosive rang once.

HALF A MILE AWAY, on the other side of the runway, at Santa Monica Airport, a sleepy security guard sat in his patrol car, smoking a cigar and watching the moon rise over Los Angeles. He was suddenly jolted fully awake by a brilliant flash across the runway, followed a millisecond later by the noise of an explosion.

He started his patrol car, switched on the flashers and the siren, and stomped on the accelerator. He crossed the runway and drove down the row of aircraft parked there, stopping fifty feet from what seemed to have been a Citation.

He got out his cell phone and dialed 911. When the operator answered he said, "This is airport security at Santa Monica Airport. An airplane has exploded, and I need the police right away. Hang on." He had spotted something lying a dozen feet from the airplane and now illuminated it with his spotlight.

It appeared to be most of a human body. "You'd better send an ambulance, too," he said. "No, on second thought, make it a coroner's hearse."

Then he hung up and pressed the speed-dial button that called his boss's home number. It rang four times before it was answered.

"What the fuck?" a sleepy voice said.

"Floyd," the security guard said, "it's Roland. You'd better get your ass over to the airport right now. We've got an exploded airplane and a dead man on our hands."

A t around seven-thirty, Stone, Ed Eagle, and Susannah Wilde were having breakfast out by the pool. Ann was sleeping in after an exciting night.

The phone buzzed next to Stone, and he picked it up. "Yes?"

"Is this Mr. Ed Eagle?"

"No, please hold." He handed the phone to Eagle. "It's for you."

Eagle pressed the instrument to his ear. "This is Ed Eagle, how can I help you?" He listened thoughtfully, a frown on his face. "You're sure it's mine?" he asked. "Yes, that's my tail number. All right, I'll be there in half an hour." He hung up and handed Stone the phone. "That was somebody with security at Santa Monica Airport," he said. "Sounds like somebody has vandalized my airplane. I'd better get a cab out there."

Stone took his last bite of omelet and put down his fork. "I'll drive you," he said. "Are your bags packed?"

"Yes, they're in the front hall."

Stone buzzed Manolo and asked him to put Mr. and Mrs. Eagle's luggage into the Arrington Cayenne parked in the driveway.

THEY WERE BUZZED through the gate at Atlantic Aviation, then met by a security car that, after ascertaining that Eagle was in the car, waved them to follow him.

Stone followed the patrol car around a large hangar and down a taxiway where a long line of airplanes was parked. A hundred yards down the taxiway were a number of vehicles— security, police, and a medical examiner's wagon. "That's a lot of attention for a vandalism call," Stone said. He pulled to a halt a few yards from the police car, and a sergeant walked over to meet them. "Mr. Ed Eagle?"

"My name is Eagle," he said, offering his hand.

"I'm afraid there's been a terrible . . . let's call it an incident— we don't really know what it is yet," the officer said.

Stone produced his NYPD badge that had been a gift of the police commissioner and that identified him as a detective first grade. "You mind if I have a look around?" he asked.

"Go ahead but be careful where you tread—as you can see, we've marked a lot of airplane pieces and body parts."

"Whose body parts?" Eagle asked.

"We don't know yet. We're about ready to search the body." He beckoned them over to where a large lump was covered by a rubber sheet. "Those of you with weak stomachs better stay back." He pulled away the sheet, revealing the torso of a good-sized man; it had only one arm and was missing a head. "Anybody any of you know?" the sergeant asked.

Everyone shook heads silently.

"Anything in his pockets?" Stone asked.

"Okay, Ralph," the sergeant said, "roll him over gently and check his pockets." Ralph did as he was told, came up with a wallet, and handed it to the sergeant. "California driver's license in the name of Harry S. Gregg. That ring a bell with anybody?"

The Eagles shook their heads, but Stone was looking thoughtful. "I've heard that name," Stone said. "Let me make a call." He got out his cell phone and pressed a button.

"Hello, Billy Burnett."

"Billy, it's Stone Barrington."

"Good morning, Stone, what can I do for you?"

"Isn't there a guy working at the Centurion armory named Gregg? He helped the president and the first lady when they were firing rifles the other day."

"Yes, Harry Gregg."

"Where are you, Billy?"

"I'm on the way to work."

"I think you'd better come to Santa Monica Airport and see what's going on here. I'm with the police at Atlantic Aviation, around the corner of a hangar from the main building, where a lot of airplanes are parked. We've got a corpse. It doesn't have a head, but a driver's license has the name Harry S. Gregg on it."

"I'll be there in fifteen minutes," Billy said.

Stone hung up. "Someone is coming who may be able to identify the body," he said to the sergeant.

"I'll be glad to see him," the sergeant replied.

"Tell me, from what you see here, what do you think happened?"

The sergeant pointed at the wrecked airplane, which Eagle was inspecting.

Stone and the sergeant walked over. "Ed, is that your airplane?" he asked.

"What's left of it," Eagle said. The nose of the airplane had disappeared, and the fuselage rested on the two main gears and the tail cone. Bits of the aircraft were scattered all over the taxiway and other airplanes, some of which were blown askew.

"Looks like the nose gear over there," the sergeant said, pointing. Stone and Eagle walked over and looked at it. Stone squatted and pointed at some duct tape. "Something was taped to the nose gear," he said, "some sort of explosive device, I should think. Sergeant, have you got anybody here from your crime lab or bomb squad?"

"On the way," the sergeant replied. They heard a vehicle approach and turned to see Billy Burnett getting out of a Mercedes station wagon.

"Good morning, Billy." Stone introduced him to the sergeant. "You know Ed Eagle, I believe."

"Sure," Billy said. He pointed at the rubber sheet. "Can I have a look?" The sheet was pulled back, and Billy squatted beside the body. He pointed at the hand of the remaining arm. "That's an army Special Forces ring," he said.

The sergeant showed him the driver's license.

"This is Harry Gregg," Billy said.

"Who was this Gregg?" the sergeant asked.

"I hired him and trained him as an armorer at the Centurion Studios armory," Billy said. "He was ex–Special Forces, a weapons and explosives expert." He looked over at Eagle's ex-airplane.

"The nose gear had some duct tape on it," Stone said, pointing at the mangled aircraft part.

"Did the body have a cell phone on it?" he asked.

"Two of them," the sergeant said, holding up an iPhone and another device.

"That one's a throwaway," Billy said, pointing at the non-Apple phone. "I think the idea was he made a bomb and attached a cell phone to it, then taped the device to the nosewheel, probably up in the wheel well. He could have set off the bomb by calling the phone taped to the device, probably after the airplane had taken off and was out over the water. My guess is somebody else called the number, probably by accident, when he had an arm and maybe his head up in the wheel well. Harry got a rude shock."

"That makes a whole lot of sense to me," the sergeant said, looking at his watch. "There'll be a couple of detectives here from our bomb squad, when they get around to it. I'd appreciate it if you'd talk to them when they get here, Mr. Burnett."

"Sure, glad to."

As if on cue, an unmarked sedan pulled up and two men in suits got out and looked around. "What a mess!" one of them said.

Detective Sergeant Chico Morales and his partner, Stockton Croft, arrived at the Venice Beach home of Harry Gregg; no one answered the door. Croft picked the lock on the front door.

"Very nice," Morales said, looking around. The house was beautifully furnished, and there was a high-end stereo system in the living room, along with a large flat-screen TV.

"He's been out of the military how long?" Croft asked.

"Less than a year, I think Burnett said."

"And he's making less than a hundred grand at the studio?"

"And driving a new pickup truck," Morales said. "I checked the title—no liens on it, so he paid cash."

"Sounds like Mr. Gregg has a business going on the side," Croft said.

They looked into the two bedrooms and found nothing of interest. In a home office, however, they found a large safe.

"We're going to have to call Tech Services and get a safe-cracker," Morales said.

"That's going to take a day or two," Croft said. "On the other hand, I know a guy."

"What the fuck, call him."

FORTY MINUTES LATER, a small man carrying a briefcase presented himself at the front door.

"Hello, Manny," Croft said. "Come take a look." He led the man into the home office.

"Fifteen minutes," Manny said. "A hundred bucks, special police rate."

"Done," Croft said, "but I'll want a receipt."

Manny inspected the lock, then pulled a stethoscope from his briefcase and pressed it against the safe door while slowly rotating the dial. "That's one," he said, turning the dial in the opposite direction. In twelve minutes, he had it open.

Croft gave him a hundred and accepted a receipt.

"You think the captain will okay that?" Morales asked.

"It's cheaper than having the LAPD do it." Croft pulled on a pair of latex gloves and opened the door. "Looka here," he said. There were half a dozen handguns of different calibers and two silencers on the shelves. There was a briefcase on the floor of the safe that, when opened, revealed a sniper rifle, broken down into parts so as to fit in the case. There was also a hefty silencer.

"It seems that Mr. Gregg offered a range of assassination services," Croft said. There was a stack of money, secured by a rubber band, and he counted it. "Thirty-nine grand," he said. There was also a plain white envelope containing only hundreds. "Twenty-five grand," he said. "I'll bet that's the first half of the payment for Eagle's airplane. We'd better check the envelope for prints."

Croft put the envelope into a plastic evidence bag. "You know," he said, "it was a good plan. Gregg could have walked down to the beach, waited for the airplane to take off, then dialed the number. The airplane would have crashed into the Pacific Ocean and broken apart. It would have taken a major operation to recover it and check for evidence, and we would have found nothing useful. But somebody dials a wrong number, and blooey! The assassin is assassinated."

"I guess we better go talk to Mrs. Grosvenor," Morales said.

"Not until we see if we can lift a print from this envelope," Morales said, holding up the evidence bag.

TWO HOURS LATER, they had a thumbprint and a name: Barbara Eagle.

"She was tried for the murder of a Mafia-connected guy at the Bel-Air Hotel," Croft said. "Thought it was Ed Eagle. She was acquitted. Weird thing is, she escaped from the court-house while the jury was deliberating and later had to plead to the escape. Let's go see her."

THEY PRESENTED THEMSELVES at the front desk of the Bel-Air Hotel and identified themselves. "Mr. and Mrs. Grosvenor checked out at eleven this morning," the desk clerk told them.

"You got a home address for them?" Morales asked.

The woman checked. "Twelve Eaton Place, London SW1," she said.

"London, England?"

"That's correct."

"Was that their destination when they checked out?"

"I assume so," she said.

"Has their room been cleaned yet?"

"I'll call housekeeping." She made the call. "Yes, and a new arrival has checked in."

Morales thanked her, and they left. "You got the address of that house in Bel-Air that the Grosvenors made an offer on?"

Croft checked his notebook. "Here we are—it's over on Copa de Oro."

"Let's see what we can find there."

THE HOUSE WAS impressive without being ostentatious. Morales rang the bell, and a uniformed houseman came to the door. Badges were flashed. "Is the owner at home?" he asked.

"Yes, sir, if you'll come in and wait a moment. He's on the tennis court, I believe."

"Just take us out there," Morales said. "What's his name?"

"Simpson," the man replied, then led the way.

Two middle-aged men were banging away on the tennis court. One of them came over after a point. "What's up?" he asked.

Badges were flashed again, and Morales introduced himself and Croft. "Mr. Simpson, I understand that you had an offer on your house from a Mr. and Mrs. Charles Grosvenor. Is that correct?"

"That is correct."

"Did you accept the offer?"

"I made a counteroffer. They wanted to think it over."

"When did you last see them?"

Simpson looked at his watch. "About an hour ago," he said.

"Do you know where they went when they left?"

"They said they were going home."

"Home to England?"

"I assume so."

"Do you happen to know on what airline they were traveling?"

"During our conversation, there was passing mention of a private jet," Simpson replied.

"Do you know what kind of jet?"

"No, but it would have to be a fairly big one for an Atlantic crossing."

"Did they mention an airport?"

"Yes, they said they were flying out of Burbank."

"Thank you, Mr. Simpson."

The two detectives left the house and headed for Burbank. Forty minutes later they were in the airport's tower.

"May I help you, gentlemen?"

"I hope so," Morales said. "Have you had a departure today of a flight to London, England?"

The man went to a computer. "Nobody would file from here to London," he said, tapping some keys. "It would likely be for a general aviation airport near London, like Cambridge or Biggin Hill." He scrolled through the flight plans on file. "Nothing for England at all."

"Maybe they were refueling and filed for someplace in between?" Croft asked.

"I've got half a dozen flight plans for Teterboro, New Jersey. That's New York."

"May I have a list of the registration numbers?" Croft asked.

The man printed them out and handed them to the detective. "There you go. I can check the registrations if you like."

"I like," Croft said.

Shortly, he was handed a list of owners of the aircraft. "They're all corporations," Croft said. "Do you have a list of the owners?"

"Afraid not," the man said. "You'll have to do a legal search. A lot of airplanes are owned by Delaware corporations. You might start there."

"Well," Morales said, "I feel a dead end coming on."

"Let's go see an ADA," Croft said. "The print might be enough for an arrest warrant, maybe even for an extradition."

"Or maybe they'll send us to London," Croft said hopefully.

Morales had a thought. "Any departures for San Francisco today?"

"Let's see," he said, sitting down at the computer again. "Oakland would be the likely destination for a general aviation aircraft." He tapped some keys. "I've got two—a Citation and a Gulfstream IV. The GIV left an hour ago."

"Gotta be the Gulfstream," Croft said. "That's a transatlantic airplane. Let's go talk to Captain Clark. He'll spring for a San Francisco trip on a crime that's getting as much TV time as this one."

S tone was back at The Arrington in time for lunch, and
he persuaded Ann to join him. He explained what had
happened to Eagle's airplane.

"The ex-wife, then?"

"Undoubtedly."

"Will the police be able to do anything?"

"They're trying, but the only material witness is dead."

"It's time we talked," Ann said. "The president left for
Washington right after breakfast this morning. Kate is waiting for the new campaign plane to be delivered—should be
here tomorrow."

"Will you have to go with her?"

"We had a long talk this morning," Ann said. "I suggested
that I might be of more use to her by continuing to work out of

the New York office. She has a good travel team without me, so she bought that."

Stone broke into a big smile. "That's wonderful news," he said. "We can fly out of here tomorrow or the next day. We're waiting for the return of the Strategic Services aircraft—it's being flown back from Tokyo. So we'll have a couple of soft days."

"Not soft for me. I'll be on the telephone constantly."

"Move into my study and work here, then. The hotel will want the presidential cottage back."

"Okay, I'll do that. Listen, the Republican convention is next week, and Senator Henry Carson of Texas looks like he's taking the nomination. Our private polls show Kate leading all the obvious Republicans, except Carson, by double digits. She's leading him by eight points."

"That's good news."

"We believe we can take him, and I've already told you what my job is going to be if that happens."

Stone nodded.

"I'll make as much time for you as I can, but I can't make any promises. If she wins, all hell will break loose the day after the election, as I'll be running the transition team."

"And I'll get to Washington as often as I can," Stone said. "Something else: I have to go to Paris this fall for the opening of the new L'Arrington there, and I have some other business there, so I may be two or three weeks. Any chance you can do some of that with me?"

"I'd love to, God knows, but I just can't manage it. I can't even say I'll try."

"Well, if that's the price of getting Kate elected, I'll just have to live with it," Stone said ruefully.

"If it's any consolation, I'll have to live with it, too," Ann said.

The phone buzzed, and Stone picked it up. "Hello?"

"Hi, it's Ed. I just wanted you to know that we made it back okay."

"I'm sorry you couldn't wait and fly with us. You'd have liked the airplane."

"I already wish we'd done that. When we got back we found my office and house staked out by the press."

"Pick somebody you like and give him an exclusive interview. Everybody else will run it, but you'll have them out of your hair."

"Good idea. I've got just the reporter in mind. Anything in particular you want me to tell them?"

"Just stick to the truth, and you won't get accused of lying to Otero and Willingham."

"Okay. Thanks for your help this morning."

"Have you heard anything new from the cops?"

"Not a word. Everybody in the world wants to talk to me but them."

"That just means they don't have anything to tell you yet."

"I guess so. Can you stop for a few days in Santa Fe on your way back?"

"I'd love to, but Ann has to get back to her New York office. She's got a lot on her plate now."

"I guess she has. Susannah sends her love. Give ours to Ann."

They hung up.

"The Eagles send love," he said to Ann.

DETECTIVES MORALES AND CROFT sat down across the desk from Captain Clark, and Croft slid a typed form across the desk.

"San Francisco?" the captain asked, feigning shock. "Is this a vacation request?"

"Cap, our only suspect is in San Francisco," Croft said. "The media are all over us on this thing, and we don't have anything to tell them."

"You actually think you're going to get something out of this Grosvenor woman?"

"We can only try."

"I remember her from her murder trial. I was the lead detective on that case, and she is the coldest, smoothest bitch I've ever laid eyes or ears on. She doesn't make mistakes."

"Nobody's lucky all the time," Morales said.

"Luck has nothing to do with it. Look, if that bomb hadn't gone off when it did, this Gregg character would have exploded it after the plane took off and we'd be right where we are now, with nothing but two waterlogged corpses. That's bad luck."

"At least we could have questioned Gregg."

"Questioned him? You wouldn't even know he existed."

"You've got a point, Cap," Croft said. "But we've gotta try to nail this woman."

"God knows I'd love to do that," Clark said. He signed the expense form and scribbled something on it. "You've got three days and my very best wishes." He slid the form back across the desk. "See the cashier, and make your travel arrangements through the department. No Ritz-Carlton."

Morales and Croft got out of there as fast as they could.

40

The Grosvenor Gulfstream IV landed smoothly at Oakland and taxied to the Business Jet Center. The stewardess took their hand luggage while the pilots and linemen moved their larger baggage from the rear compartment to their Bentley Mulsanne, which stood, idling, beside the big jet.

"Anything I need to know about the last twenty-four hours?" Charles asked as he helped Barbara into her coat.

"Nothing you *want* to know," she said, pecking him on the lips. "Just remember I haven't been out of your sight the past couple of days, except to go to the hotel salon."

They walked down the airstair door and into the Bentley.

"Home, James," Charles said to their driver, whose name was actually James. He had been invalided out of a career as a pro football linebacker by a knee injury during his fourth season and was now a factotum for the Grosvenors.

James delivered them to their apartment on Green Street, just off Nob Hill, and they took the elevator to the penthouse while James and the doormen dealt with the luggage.

Charles called his dealership and got a report from the sales manager, then he hung up. "We sold two Flying Spurs and a Mulsanne while we were gone, and four used vehicles. I wish Bentley would deliver new cars at the factory in England— we'd sell four or five more a year to people who want to tour in their new cars."

"Keep after them, Charles," Barbara said. She turned to the maid who was unpacking her bags. "Run me a bath."

LATE IN THE afternoon Chico Morales and Stockton Croft got off a flight at San Francisco International that had been somewhat less comfortable than the Grosvenor Gulfstream. They picked up their plain, underpowered rental car and drove to their blank-faced business hotel on an unfashionable block off California Street. There was no valet service or doorman, so they had to park on the street and carry their own luggage, after Croft had extracted a police placard from his briefcase and slipped it over a sun visor. He hoped the meter maid wouldn't notice that the badge it displayed was from L.A.

"So, what's your plan?" Morales asked.

"I don't have a plan," Croft replied.

"You always have a plan."

"I have a dinner plan, but not a work plan—until tomorrow morning. I know a good restaurant that won't shock our cashier when we turn in our expenses."

"I place myself in your hands," Morales said.

"Smart move."

They dined at the bar at the Huntington Hotel, a block away from theirs, and failed to pick up anybody.

Barbara and Charles Grosvenor dined on their terrace, which had a sweeping view of San Francisco Bay.

"We're having such beautiful weather," Barbara said. "I thought I'd run up to Napa for a couple of days." They had a house in the wine country outside St. Helena. "Would you like to come?"

"I really should spend the time at the dealership, my darling," Charles replied. "It does need my attention after a week away. You go and enjoy yourself."

BILLY BURNETT SAT in the restaurant at the Huntington Hotel and spotted the two Los Angeles detectives immediately as they came into the bar. Billy's presence was partially screened by a potted plant, and anyway, even people who had met him rarely noticed him in such circumstances, since he was not a noticeable person, and in any case, he had selected a hairpiece and mustache from his makeup case, and he wore glasses he did not need.

Billy had spent much of his day searching databases not available to the public. He could log on to the CIA mainframe and from there enter virtually any other computer in the country while leaving no trace of his visit. He had compiled quite a dossier on Barbara Eagle and her British husband; he was getting to know them quite well. They had a house in London, an apartment in New York, a place in Palm Springs, and a house in Napa, in addition to their Green Street apartment. He had obtained the tail number of their Gulfstream from the tower computer at Burbank earlier in the day and had lifted their flight plan. He had landed his own airplane, a JetPROP—a single-engine turboprop—at Hayward, on the eastern shore of the bay, south of Oakland, and checked into the Huntington, using a credit card and a California driver's license in another name, part of his little inventory of identities.

Tomorrow, Billy would do some scouting around, then, perhaps, pay Mrs. Grosvenor a visit. He looked forward to meeting her.

MORALES AND CROFT ambled back to their hotel and, along the way, spotted a parking ticket on their rental car. Written across the bottom of the ticket were the words *Welcome to San Francisco, schmuck!*

"I never liked this town," Croft said.

T he following morning Morales and Croft had breakfast in their hotel's restaurant, since their room was too
small to contain both them and a room service cart.
Morales was reading something.

"What's that?" Croft asked.

"It was attached to our travel order. It's about how to be a
good police visitor to another city, and it has a number for us
to call and check in with the SFPD."

"Fuck 'em," Croft said.

Morales got out his cell phone, called the number, and
introduced himself, then he hung up.

"That was short."

"We have to go to the Central Station, show our badges, and
check in personally."

"Fuck 'em," Croft said again.

"They already have our names, sent from L.A.," Morales pointed out. "And if we check in, they'll give us an SFPD ID and a parking pass for the city streets."

"Do we *both* have to go?"

"If we do, we won't get into trouble for impersonating police officers."

"We *are* police officers."

"Not in San Francisco, until we check in."

THEY FOUND THE Central Station on Vallejo Street and presented themselves at the front desk, where they were directed upstairs to a room number. They knocked and entered.

"Okay, where you from?" a woman in civilian clothes said without looking up from her desk.

"Los Angeles," Morales replied.

"Swell," she said. "Badges and ID?" She took them to a Xerox machine and made a copy. "Go stand against the wall, there, one at a time."

They did so and were photographed.

"How long you here for?"

"Five days," Croft said, just in case.

She typed something into a computer and pressed a button; a moment later a machine next to her desk vomited two plastic cards with their badges and ID on one side and an SFPD star on the other, plus the banner VISITING OFFICER. She gave them each a clip that allowed them to fasten the cards to their lapels. "Wear 'em when you're in any police station or questioning anybody in this city." She handed them a parking pass for their car. "That may keep you from getting a ticket. On the other hand, it may get your car vandalized."

"Thanks very much."

"Don't mention it." She had never once looked at them.

"We could be Bonnie and Clyde, and she wouldn't know the difference," Croft said as the door closed behind them.

BILLY BURNETT ARRIVED on Green Street and found a parking place, then he went and had a look at Barbara Eagle's apartment building. Elegant. As he watched, a white Bentley Mulsanne drove up to the entrance. The driver popped the trunk lid, then got out. Billy made him to be six-five and close to three hundred pounds, but his waist was slim. A blunt instrument. A doorman appeared with a small bag and a train case and set them in the trunk. He pressed a button, and the trunk lid closed itself.

Barbara Eagle appeared, dressed in slacks and a sweater set, an impressive double string of pearls around her neck, and got into the waiting car. Blunt Instrument got in and drove away.

Billy ran the few steps back to his car, got it started, and followed. As he drove down the street, a car containing the two L.A. detectives passed, going the other way.

MORALES AND CROFT pulled up to the entrance to the building and got out. They showed their new guest IDs to the doorman. "We'd like to see Mrs. Charles Grosvenor," Morales said.

"You just missed her," the doorman said. "She's headed to Napa for a few days."

"What's the address?"

"Beats me."

"What's she driving?" Croft asked.

"She's *being* driven," the doorman replied, "in a white Bentley. A big one." He pointed down the street.

The two detectives looked and saw the car turning a corner. They dived back into their car and followed. As they turned the corner they could see the Bentley two blocks ahead.

"At least it's easy to spot," Morales said.

"Will this thing go any faster?" Croft asked.

Morales stomped on the accelerator. Hardly anything happened.

"Shit," Croft said, "we didn't check out of the hotel. What are we going to do for clothes?"

"I always keep a clean shirt and socks and some paper boxer shorts in my briefcase, just in case," Morales said. "Toothbrush and razor, too."

"*Paper* boxer shorts?"

"You just throw 'em away when you're done with 'em."

"Sometimes I hate your guts, you know that?"

BILLY SAW THE cops' rental car, a small red Korean vehicle, in his rearview mirror. He opened his briefcase and took out a little stack of papers. On top was the address of the Napa house. He headed for Hayworth Airport.

"FOR A MINUTE, I thought that silver BMW was following the Bentley," Morales said, "but he turned left."

"Are you getting paranoid on the lady's behalf?" Croft asked.

"Just being observant. They taught us that at the academy, or did you miss that day?"

BILLY TURNED IN his rental car at the Hayward FBO and filed an IFR flight plan to Napa County Airport. It wasn't far, but going IFR would help him deal with the controllers. He did a quick preflight, then got the airplane started and asked for his clearance and permission to taxi. Shortly, he was airborne, and the ATC controllers vectored him around and out of the busy San Francisco Class B area. He had been in the air for only twelve minutes when he spotted Napa County. He pressed the transmit button on the yoke. "I have the airport in sight. I'll cancel IFR at this time." The controller said goodbye and Billy descended for his landing.

He rented another car, this one a brand-new Chevrolet Impala, which impressed him, and he drove to St. Helena. He found the Grosvenors' house, a handsome, shingle-style McMansion on a little hill, then he parked in a partially hidden road across from it. Twenty minutes later, the white Mulsanne appeared, followed by the red Korean car containing the two policemen. The Bentley turned into the driveway, drove through some trees, and appeared on the hill in front of the house, where Barbara exited while Blunt Instrument retrieved her minimal luggage.

The Korean car drove slowly past the house.

"What do you want to do now?" Morales asked.

"Let's give her time to settle in before we knock on the door," Croft said. "In the meantime, let's go back to St. Helena and find a men's store."

"Did you see the new Impala parked in the side road?"

"Yeah, what about it?"

"Two things: it's the new model, which is getting rave reviews, and the guy inside was driving the silver BMW back in the city."

"You're nuts. How could he beat us here and be in another car?"

"I'm just observing," Morales said. "I haven't figured that out yet."

42

L ate in the day, Stone's curiosity got the better of him. He called the West Los Angeles LAPD station and asked for Detective Morales. The extension rang, and a male voice answered. "Homicide. Detective Angelo."

"May I speak with either Detective Morales or Detective Croft?" Stone asked.

"They're out of the city on a case," the man replied. "May I help you?"

"Thank you, no," Stone replied, and hung up. He called Peter's office and asked for Billy Burnett.

"I'm sorry," a woman said, "he's out with the flu, probably for a few days."

Stone thanked her, hung up, and called Billy's cell number.

"Billy Burnett," a voice said.

"It's Stone Barrington. I'm sorry to hear you're ill."

"Thanks, Stone, but I'm fine."

"I just wondered if you'd heard anything from Morales or Croft."

"Not a word," Billy said, "but they've gone to San Francisco to talk with her."

"How do you know that?" Stone asked.

Billy looked up and saw the red Korean car, which had been gone for nearly an hour, approaching the Grosvenor house again. "Trust me," Billy said. "You're going to have to excuse me, Stone. I'll call you tomorrow." He hung up without waiting for a reply. He watched as the little car turned into the Grosvenor driveway.

MORALES AND CROFT followed the long driveway through some trees and up a hill and came to a halt in front of the house. "Nice place," Morales said.

"Let's get in there and brace her," Croft said, opening the door.

"Shall we use our new SFPD ID?" Morales asked.

"We're not in SF anymore," Croft replied, ringing the bell.

A huge young man in a well-cut suit came to the door. "Good afternoon," he said. "How may I help you?"

The two detectives flashed badges. "We'd like to speak with Mrs. Grosvenor," Morales said.

"May I know the nature of your business?"

"It's police business," Croft replied. "Tell her that."

"Please come in," the man said, stepping out of their way and indicating that they should go into a room to their left. "Please have a seat. I'll let her know you're here."

He left and the detectives found themselves in a handsome library, with shelves lined with leather-bound books. Croft took one off a shelf and looked at it. "Winston Churchill," he said. He replaced the book.

"Good afternoon, gentlemen," Barbara Grosvenor said, in her pleasant, well-modulated voice.

They turned to find an elegantly dressed woman with straight gray hair to her shoulders. "Good afternoon, Mrs. Grosvenor," Morales said.

"Won't you please sit down?"

They both sat on a sofa, and she took a chair opposite them. "Would you like some refreshment?" she asked. "It's late in the day—perhaps something more substantial?"

"Anything soft would be very nice," Morales said.

Barbara lifted a phone on the table next to her and said, "May we have a pitcher of iced tea, please?" She hung up. "It won't be a moment. I understand you're from Los Angeles, is that correct?"

"That is correct," Morales said. "We're conducting an investigation, and we think you can help us."

She started to speak, but a uniformed houseman entered the room and set a pitcher of iced tea, three glasses, and a plate of cookies on the coffee table before them.

"Thank you, Benito," Barbara said.

He poured the tea, then left. Everyone took a sip of iced tea.

"Excellent," Morales said.

Croft let Morales do the talking; he took a cookie and watched the woman closely.

"An investigation?" Barbara said. "What sort of investigation?"

"Early this morning, before dawn, an airplane exploded at Santa Monica Airport. Perhaps you saw something about it on TV."

"No, I haven't seen a TV all day. Was anyone hurt?"

"Only the man who placed the bomb in the nose of the airplane," Morales said. He decided not to tell her Gregg was dead.

"I'm a little confused," Barbara said. "Why would you come all the way to Napa to ask me about the explosion of an airplane?"

"The airplane belonged to your ex-husband, Ed Eagle," Morales said.

"And Ed wasn't harmed?"

"No, he had not yet arrived at the airport."

"How unfortunate," she said with a smile.

"I take it you and your ex-husband are not on good terms."

"I wouldn't know, I haven't seen him in years, and I was married to someone else after Ed and before Mr. Grosvenor. My former husband died in an automobile accident."

"Mrs. Grosvenor, are you acquainted with an employee of Centurion Studios named Harry Gregg?"

"I don't think so. Is he a producer there?"

Nice touch, Morales thought. "No, he worked in the armory, where the studio keeps weapons used in films."

"I have an investment in Centurion Studios, but I have visited the place only once, for a stockholders' meeting a few years ago. The only person I know there is Leo Goldman Junior, who is the chief executive."

"I see," Morales said. "Before we go any further, Mrs. Grosvenor, I'm required by law to read you your rights." He took a card from his pocket and did so. "Do you wish to have an attorney present while I question you?"

"My goodness, no. Why would I need an attorney present?" Barbara said.

"As you wish, Mrs. Grosvenor. Now, I should tell you that Harry Gregg had placed the bomb in the airplane and, while he was doing so, the bomb exploded, killing Mr. Gregg instantly."

"Poor Mr. Gregg," Barbara said, with ironic sympathy.

"In our investigation of the explosion we visited Mr. Gregg's home in Venice and searched it thoroughly," Morales said. "During the search we opened a safe in his home office and found multiple weapons and a great deal of cash."

Barbara stared at him blankly and shrugged, as if to say, "Why do I care?"

"Twenty-five thousand dollars of the cash was in a plain white envelope, which we believe was a partial payment for the planting of the bomb in Mr. Eagle's airplane. We found your thumbprint on that envelope."

Shit! Barbara thought, but her face betrayed only curiosity.

"Heavens, why would my fingerprint be on an envelope in the home of this person—Mr. Gregg, was it?"

"Correct. We were hoping you could answer that question. Why was your fingerprint on that envelope?"

Barbara looked baffled. "I haven't the foggiest idea," she said. "Isn't that the sort of thing you gentlemen are supposed to find out?"

"It is," Morales said.

"Well, when you do, I shall be very curious to learn how that happened."

"We are inclined to think that your fingerprint was placed on the envelope when you handed it to Mr. Gregg," Morales said.

Croft watched the woman with fascination, but he said nothing.

"Gentlemen, let me be perfectly clear," Barbara said. "I do not now nor have I ever known this Mr. Gregg, and so it follows that I have never handed him an envelope, let alone one containing money."

"Mrs. Grosvenor, we are aware that you have been accused of murder in the past."

"Then you must be aware that I was found innocent," she replied smoothly. "Gentlemen, I must lay all of this at the feet of my former husband, Mr. Eagle. He has been saying for years that I am trying to kill him, when nothing could be further from the truth. I'm afraid that, during all that time, I am told by professionals, he has exhibited symptoms of severe paranoia. I have nothing to gain from his death. We have been divorced for many years, and I asked nothing of him at that time. I am very much more wealthy than he, so there could be no financial motive, and I bear him no ill will, except for these ridiculous charges of his, for which there has never been a shred of proof. I'm very much afraid that the best explanation for this airplane explosion is that Mr. Eagle hired this Mr. Gregg to blow it up, so that he could make yet another baseless charge against me."

"Then how do you explain the fingerprint on the envelope?"

"When Mr. Eagle and I were married, I often typed correspondence for him. It is entirely possible, even likely, that he possessed an envelope bearing my fingerprint, one that he has preserved for this special occasion. Now, have you any other questions for me? I'm expecting guests for dinner, and I have to consult with the cook about the menu and then change."

"No, Mrs. Grosvenor," Morales said. "We have no other questions—at this time. But you may expect to see us again."

Barbara stood up, and the detectives stood with her. "Then I bid you good evening, gentlemen."

The large young man had appeared silently at the door to the library, and he escorted them to the front door. "Good evening, gentlemen," he said, closing it behind them.

"Well," Croft said, "Captain Clark was right—she is the coldest, smoothest bitch ever to come down the pike."

"Yes," Morales said, "and she blew our fingerprint evidence right out of the water. Given her reasoning, it would never convict her."

"I'd like to make a prediction," Croft said. "Nobody is ever going to convict that woman of anything."

They drove down the driveway to the road. "We may as well go back to San Francisco for the night," Morales said. "It's only an hour and a half or so, and we're done here."

"So I won't need my new shirt and shorts?"

"No. By the way, did you notice that the Impala driven by the man from San Francisco was still parked in the side road?"

"Will you stop it with this observation crap, Chico? There's no way that guy could have got here and changed cars!"

Billy Burnett saw them head back toward St. Helena, and he continued to wait quietly for darkness to fall.

Morales and Croft got back to their hotel, cleaned up, then went back to the Huntington Hotel bar and settled down with drinks. Five minutes later, two very attractive young women who appeared to be in their early thirties came in and took the only two stools vacant, which happened to be right next to Croft.

"Evening," Croft said. "Can I get you two ladies a drink?"

The two looked him up and down, then one of them said, "Why not? Two Tito's martinis, straight up, with a fistful of olives."

The drinks arrived, and everyone toasted and drank. "I'm Stockton Croft, and this is my partner, Chico Morales."

"I'm Pam Hale, and this is Sherry Tate," the blonder of the two said. "What are you two partners in?"

"Crime fighting," Croft said. "We're LAPD detectives."

"Ah," Pam said, "and what brings you all the way to San Francisco?"

"The investigation of an attempted murder and an inadvertent suicide," Croft replied. "What do you two do?"

"I do news features on the six o'clock news at WSFO," Pam said, "and Sherry is the weather girl."

"The *meteorologist*," Sherry said.

"Sorry, Sherry. Tell me about your crime, Stockton—what was it again?"

"Attempted murder and inadvertent suicide."

"That sounds fascinating. Tell me everything."

"Well, this guy who works at a movie studio got hired to kill a lawyer who is a pilot, so he went out to Santa Monica Airport and packed half a pound of plastic explosives into the nosewheel well of a Citation and attached the detonator to a cell phone."

"So the guy could call the number and the bomb would go off?"

"Exactly, except the guy got unlucky. Somebody called the number of the cell phone—probably a misdial—and the bomb went off while the guy was installing it."

"And what did that do to the guy?"

"Blew off his head and one arm, and badly damaged his dignity."

The girls winced and laughed. "And thus," Pam said, "attempted murder and inadvertent suicide!"

"Right you are."

"I love it, but how did it get you to San Francisco?"

"We came up to question a suspect."

"But the suspect is dead."

"The person who hired the suspect is not dead."

"Ah, and who is he?"

"She."

"Who?"

"No names," Morales said suddenly, speaking for the first time. "She's only a suspect at this point."

"A woman hired this guy?"

"We're pretty sure she did," Croft said, "but we don't have enough evidence to nail her—yet."

"Wow! So this is an ongoing investigation!"

"That's exactly what it is."

"You know, this is exactly the kind of story I cover," Pam said. "I'd love to interview this lady."

"Oh, I don't think she wants any publicity," Croft said. "She's a prominent person in your city—serves on a bunch of charity and arts boards, gives away millions."

"Oh, come on, Stockton . . ."

"Call me Stock—everybody does."

"Stock, tell me all the details, and I'm buying dinner. There's a very good restaurant right over there." She pointed across the bar.

Croft looked at Morales. "That's a pretty good offer, Chico. What do you think?"

"Sounds great, but no names."

"We'll see about that after a bottle of good wine," Pam said, waving at the headwaiter and holding up four fingers.

——————

BILLY WAITED UNTIL the last vestiges of the sunset had gone, then started his car. Then he turned it off again. A car's headlights were turning into the Grosvenors' driveway, and a moment later two other cars arrived. The front door of the house was opened, and half a dozen people were admitted.

Billy switched on the ignition and brought up the car's navigator. He pressed the button that showed him his position, then cranked the zoom knob until he had a large-scale map of the immediate area. It took only a moment to find what he was looking for. To his left, another road turned off the main highway, then intersected with yet another road that ran behind the Grosvenor property. He started the car again and pulled into the main road, then took two rights, keeping the house on his right. As he made the second right, he turned off the headlights and stopped at a wide place in the road.

Billy got out of the car, took off his tan windbreaker, and turned it inside out, making it black. He put on a black knitted cap, as well, then checked his little 9mm semiautomatic and returned it to its holster, then he closed the car door, climbed over a fence, and began walking toward the house.

As he did, he screwed a silencer into the barrel of his weapon.

44

By the time the first course arrived, the four had, by common consent, divided into two couples. Croft got Pam, Morales got Sherry, and everyone seemed happy with that.

The bottle of wine Pam had selected arrived and was poured, then glasses were clinked.

"Now," Pam said, taking a bite of her pâté and leaning forward, "tell me everything."

Croft took a deep breath and started into Barbara Eagle's history of trying to murder her husband, while Pam listened avidly and Sherry and Chico mumbled to each other. When Croft had finished, Pam said, "Wow."

BILLY BURNETT MOVED through some trees and plantings behind the house until he could see people entering a room at a rear corner and sitting down. Dinner, he supposed. He ran the last few yards to the house, broke through some bordering shrubs, and knelt down, listening. Nothing: no alarms, no footsteps, no dogs. He rolled down his knitted cap, which covered his face but left openings for eyes and mouth, then, carefully, he stood up and looked in the window.

Seven people were around a round table, and Barbara's back was toward Billy. He unzipped his fanny pack, took out a small battery-operated amplifier, plugged a cord into it, then he licked a suction cup, stuck it to the window, and put an earbud into one ear. They were, apparently, continuing a conversation begun in the living room over drinks.

"I TELL YOU," Barbara was saying, "Ed Eagle has made my life hell for years. He's made at least four attempts on my life, then blamed me for trying to kill him. The latest you may have seen on TV. He hired someone to plant a bomb on his airplane, and the man cocked it up somehow and blew himself up, as well. Then, of course, he told the Los Angeles police that I had hired someone to kill him. Two LAPD detectives were here until an hour before you all arrived, questioning me."

"Why don't you sue Eagle?" one of the women asked.

"What for? I don't want or need his money, and, anyway, Ed is one of the best trial lawyers in the country. It would cost me millions, then nothing would happen."

"Why don't you go public, then?" the man asked.

"Jack, what do you mean by 'go public'?"

"Take the offensive—give a few, select interviews to the right members of the press, and turn the whole thing back on Eagle. Show him up for the villain he is, ruin his reputation, cost him clients. Maybe he'd get the message then."

"I never thought of that," Barbara said. "But I wouldn't have a clue how to go about it."

"A good friend of mine, Hugh Gordon, is the top publicist in the city," Jack said.

"But I'm not selling anything," Barbara replied. "I haven't written a book or anything like that."

"You're selling your story, nothing else. Of course, a book might come later. Hugh would know exactly how to handle this situation. He knows every important journalist on the West Coast, and a lot in New York, too. If you like, I'll have him call you tomorrow. You could discuss it with him and, if you feel it's the right thing to do, come up with a plan."

"Perhaps I should at least talk to him," Barbara said.

BILLY HEARD a noise. He wasn't sure what it was, but it was enough for him to pocket his listening gear and sit very still, huddled next to the house, behind bushes. As he continued to listen, he heard soft footsteps approaching, and a powerful beam of light began flitting around the rear of the house. Billy curled into a ball, his head tucked against his knees, exposing only black to the approaching threat.

"I know you're here," a voice said. "You didn't count on our security system, did you? I'm armed, and unless you come out and identify yourself, I'm going to start firing randomly into the shrubbery."

Billy uncoiled, stood up, and saw a very large man—Blunt Instrument. He had read about him in his research: ex-NFL player, knee injury. Billy walked confidently toward him, and the man raised his pistol. Billy slowed, but continued, doing what his opponent had not expected, coming closer.

"Hold it right there," the man said.

Billy took one step closer to him and swung the edge of his left hand at the man's right wrist. The pistol flew out of the man's hand. He emitted a short cry of pain, then Billy kicked him, not too hard, in his right knee, and the man collapsed and held the knee.

"That's the correct knee, isn't it? If I encounter you again, I'll ruin it permanently for you. It will take you months to get over the surgery. And you would be wise not to mention this little tiff to your mistress."

Billy turned and walked toward his car, picking up the man's weapon along the way and tossing it as far as he could into the darkness. He looked back once and saw the man still lying on the ground, clutching his knee.

S tone and Ann were at lunch the following day, when Mike Freeman called. Stone spoke to him briefly, then hung up.

"The Strategic Services G650 will be ready for us tomorrow morning at ten," he said.

"Oh, good," Ann said. "And when I get back all hell will have broken loose, and it will remain loose until the election, then a different kind of hell will break loose, assuming Kate wins. Then, on January twentieth a special kind of hell will await me. Everyone who has ever held this job has said that it was the hardest work and the toughest job they ever had."

"You sound as though you're reconsidering," Stone said hopefully.

"On the contrary, I can't wait to get started," she said.

Stone laughed. "Kate is lucky to have you." The phone rang, and he picked it up. "Yes?"

"It's Billy."

"Hi there. Feeling better?"

"As good as new," Billy said, "but shortly, Ed Eagle is going to be feeling a lot worse."

"Oh, God," Stone said, "is there another attempt coming?"

"Not on his life—on his reputation."

"What do you mean?"

"Barbara is hiring a press agent in San Francisco named Hugh Gordon. I checked him out. He's among the two or three best publicists in the country, and he's arranging a series of interviews in which Barbara will insist that Eagle is trying to kill *her*. She's going to blindside him, and he'll never be able to catch up."

"Oh, shit! What should I tell him to do?"

"This is outside my area of expertise, but I should think the only thing he can do is beat her to the punch."

"Thanks, Billy. How did you find out about this?"

"Don't ask, and don't tell Eagle this came from me."

"All right." Stone thanked him again, hung up, and called Ed Eagle.

"Good morning, Mr. Barrington. I'm afraid Ed is in court this morning, but he should be breaking for lunch soon, and he'll call in for messages."

"Please ask Ed to call me first," Stone said. "It's extremely urgent that I talk to him at the earliest possible moment."

"I'll certainly do that, Mr. Barrington."

Stone hung up. "Who do you know in the New York press?" he asked Ann.

"Are you kidding? *Everybody.*"

Stone explained the call he'd just had. "Who are the top people he should talk to?"

"In New York?"

"National."

"Well, the plum pick is *60 Minutes*, but even if they want the story, it might take some time, at the very least, to get it on the air. I know the executive producer, and he owes me a favor. After that, the morning shows—*Today*, *CBS This Morning*, *Good Morning America*, CNN, and *Morning Joe*."

The phone rang. "Stone Barrington."

"Stone, it's Ed. Are you in some sort of trouble?"

"No, Ed, you are."

"Gee, I hadn't noticed."

"I've just received some information that you have to act on at once."

"What kind of information?"

"Barbara has decided, in lieu of killing you, to wage war on you through the media. She's hired a top publicist, and he's arranging press and TV interviews for her now. She's going to say that you've been trying to kill her and then blaming it on her."

"How the hell did you hear about this?"

"I can't reveal my source, but I can tell you that this is real, and you have to attack first."

"How'm I supposed to do that?"

"Hire your own publicist and beat her to the punch."

"Well, Susannah has a publicist, of course—all the Holly-wood folks do. I could talk to him."

"Ann is here. She knows the executive producer of *60 Min-utes*, and she's willing to call him on your behalf. Tell your publicist that. You need to work out a plan with your guy both to punch and counterpunch. You've got to have an argument ready for every point she makes. And speaking as an attorney, you'd better be ready for a slander suit once she hears what you're doing. She can outspend you."

"Well, then, I'm going to have to let her throw the first punch," Ed said. "After that, I'll just be defending myself."

"That won't be enough, Ed, you're going to have to destroy her, burn her to the ground."

Ed was silent for a moment. "I can't say I relish that thought," he said.

"If you don't do it to her, she's going to do it to you. She'll ruin your practice. And, while she's at it, ruin your life."

"She's certainly capable of that."

"She's crazy, Ed, and you're going to have to be the sane, sensible one while she's making the wild allegations. You've got one important thing going for you: there's a record of the things she's done—her prison sentence as an accessory to murder, her theft of your money and escape to Mexico, the conviction down there of killing a policeman, her escape from a Mexican prison, and then the shooting at the Bel-Air. You're going to have to turn her acquittal into a miscarriage of justice."

"That's exactly what it was," Ed said. "I was astonished

when she walked. I've also got the knife attack on me and the time I spent in the hospital on my side. Nobody has ever hurt Barbara."

"It's time to call Susannah's publicist, and you'd better get some cash together, because hiring a publicist and conducting this kind of campaign is going to cost as much as it would cost to hire you to defend somebody."

"I'd better get on it, then."

"Keep me posted?"

"Sure."

"I'll be back in New York tomorrow night." Stone hung up.

"I expect that call scared the shit out of Ed," Ann said. "It certainly would me."

"He's taking it seriously. Luckily, Susannah already has a publicist."

"Let me know when you want me to call *60 Minutes*," Ann said.

PAM HALE SAT in her cubicle at WSFO in San Francisco and read the transcript of Barbara Eagle's murder trial in Los Angeles. Her friend Sherry, the meteorologist, stopped by. "You've been intense all morning," she said. "What's up?"

"I'm just reading about this woman, Barbara Eagle—or rather, Grosvenor."

"Could you believe it when Chico told us her name? She's all over everywhere in this town."

"I'm just reading the transcript of her murder trial. She

must have had one hell of a lawyer to get off." Pam's phone rang, and she picked it up. "Pam Hale, talk fast."

A man laughed. "Pam, it's Hugh Gordon. How are you?"

"Just great, Hugh. How do I rate a phone call from the Great Gordon?"

He laughed again.

"You've got to be pitching something."

"This is more in the nature of a public service," Gordon said. "An acquaintance of mine, a woman of unimpeachable character, a patron of the arts and a philanthropist, is being pursued by her ex-husband, who has made repeated attempts on her life."

"Gee, Hugh, that sounds just awful. Who is she?"

"Before I can tell you that, I want to know if you'll interview her for your weekend show."

"I can't tell you that until I know who she is, Hugh."

"So we're at loggerheads?"

"Come on, Hugh, you can't expect me to commit to a major interview with someone whose name I don't know."

"All right, but this is in the strictest confidence."

"Of course, Hugh, it always is."

"Her name is Barbara Grosvenor, formerly Barbara Eagle."

"Oh, sure, she's social dynamite with all that money. Who's trying to kill her?"

"The ex-husband's name is Ed Eagle. He's a big-time attorney out of Santa Fe, does a lot of trial work on the West Coast."

"I'll Google him and see what I find."

"You won't get the good stuff on Google—you'll get that only from interviewing Barbara."

"Okay, I'm in," Pam said. "I'll have to talk to my producer, but he pretty much follows my lead."

"Call me back within the hour, and we'll schedule." Gordon hung up.

Pam hung up, too. "You're not going to believe this," she said to Sherry. "Hugh Gordon is flogging interviews with the lady! Excuse me," she said, getting up and smoothing her skirt. "I've got to run this by Ron right now to get her on the weekend show." She took off, running down the hallway.

46

L ate in the afternoon, as Stone was reading a book in
his library, the phone rang, and he picked up. "Stone
Barrington."

"It's Ed. I just want you to know that I've already
hired a publicist, and he's coming to Santa Fe tomorrow with a
camera crew."

"That sounds great, Ed."

"What we're going to do is a long interview that can be cut
up to address different points, as a way of defending myself.
I'm also doing another long interview that will address Barbara's history of murderous conduct, her convictions, her
prison sentences, and her changes of identity over the years.
Depending on what she has to say in her first interview, we
can be on the air immediately by sending TV stations all or
part of the two interviews. Also, the publicist, whose name is

Hal Henry, wants me to tell you to tell Ann to go ahead and call *60 Minutes*. She can tell the executive producer that they can review all the tapes we're making and use as much or as little as they like, or they can send a correspondent out here to do their own interview, or I'll go to New York and be interviewed there. I am at their disposal."

"Sounds like you're ready for anything," Stone said. "I'll talk to Ann at dinner and ask her to phone *60 Minutes* first thing in the morning."

"That's wonderful, Stone. Thank you, and please thank Ann for me, too. Now I've got to go and talk to Susannah—she's writing a rough draft of what I'm going to say."

"Ed, my advice, for what it's worth, is don't read from a script. You're used to talking on your feet. Review your points and sell it like a closing argument."

"That's good advice, Stone, and I'll take it."

"And if you come to New York for interviews, I insist you and Susannah stay with me and, if you like, record interviews there."

"That sounds perfect. I'll keep you posted." Eagle hung up as Ann entered the room. "That was Ed Eagle. He's hired a publicist named Hal Henry, and he wants you to call your contact at *60 Minutes*." Stone told her about Ed's plans to record interviews. "Can you call him first thing tomorrow morning?"

Ann looked at her watch. "He's a late worker, I'll try him now." She sat down in the chair next to Stone's and picked up the phone. Stone went to fix them a drink, and when he came back, she was just hanging up.

Stone handed her a drink. "How'd that go?"

"Amazingly well," Ann said. "One of his producers has already had a call from a publicist in San Francisco named Hugh Gordon, shopping the piece."

"Uh-oh."

"But there's a twist," she said. "They've also had a call from an interviewer named Pam Hale, at an independent TV station in San Francisco, who has an interview with Barbara scheduled for tomorrow and an exclusive in her market. The twist is, she's already researched Barbara's background, and she plans to let her make her case, then hit her with some hard questions. She's offered her raw footage to *60 Minutes*, and they're very interested."

"That sounds good," Stone said.

"They did a piece on Ed some years ago, about a trial he was conducting, and they like him. They'd like him to come to New York tomorrow and to be available for interviews."

Stone picked up the phone, called Eagle, and told him about Ann's conversation with *60 Minutes*. "If you want to do it, we'll pick you and Susannah up in Santa Fe at around eleven your time tomorrow morning and take you with us."

"Hang on," Ed said, then put him on hold. He came back a moment later. "We're on," he said. "Susannah has told the publicist, and she thinks he should come, too. Have you got room for him and an assistant on the airplane?"

"Plenty of room," Stone said. "Have him meet us at Atlantic Aviation at Burbank tomorrow morning at ten, and I'll be happy to put them up at my house."

"He'll be there," Ed replied. "See you here tomorrow at eleven."

"Bye." Stone hung up, called Mike Freeman, and told him what was up. "Can you handle the four extra passengers, Mike? Dino and Viv left after the convention. If it's a problem, please say so and I'll charter something."

"No problem at all, Stone. You always bring along such interesting people. I'll see you at the airport, and I'll let our pilot know to include Santa Fe in his flight planning."

Stone hung up and called Joan Robertson. "It's Stone. Sorry to call so late."

"Hey, there. You still coming home tomorrow?"

"Yes, and I'm bringing four guests: Ed Eagle and his wife, Susannah Wilde, a publicist named Hal Henry and his assistant. Please have the second-floor suite freshened up for the Eagles and two rooms on the third floor for Henry and his assistant."

"Will do. What time will you be in?"

Stone did some rough mental calculations with flight times and time zones. "We should be at the house between four and five. Send Fred and the Bentley for us and the Eagles, and another car and driver for the publicists."

"I can do that."

"And tell Helene we'll be six or eight for dinner tomorrow night."

"Right. Anything else?"

"I'll call you from the airplane if I think of anything else." Stone hung up. "I think we're all set," Stone said.

Ann looked at him. "I'm impressed with your organizing skills," she said. "How would you like to work on Kate's campaign full-time?"

"Thanks, but I still practice a little law now and then, and Woodman and Weld are wondering where the hell I've been for the past ten days."

S tone, Ann, the publicist Hal Henry, and his assistant, who turned out to be a beautiful blonde of about twenty-five named Tina, took off from Burbank Airport a little after ten A.M. and were soon cleared direct to Santa Fe, with a detour over the Grand Canyon that Stone had requested.

As they approached the Canyon, Stone told everyone to raise their window blinds. The view from the G650's big windows was spectacular.

"You know," Ann said, "I've never seen it before. It's so much bigger than I realized."

"Yes. And if we hadn't been doing six hundred knots over the ground with a tailwind, it would have seemed even bigger."

The big jet set down at Santa Fe and, with its large tanks,

didn't need refueling. The pilot shut down the engine on the side of the airplane with the door and Ed, Suzannah, and their luggage were aboard in less than a minute while the copilot got their clearance for Teterboro. The pilot restarted the engine and they were wheels-up after a stop of less than fifteen minutes.

The stewardess served them a lunch of lobster salad with a Cakebread Chardonnay from California, and they were on the ground at Teterboro a little after four. Rush-hour traffic was heavy, but they were at Stone's house at five-thirty, where Fred and the driver of the other car got their luggage into the house.

"Everybody freshen up and get some rest, if you like," Stone said to his guests. "Drinks are at seven, with dinner to follow."

"Dino called and asked if he could bring a couple of guests," Joan said, as she gave Stone his messages. "I've alerted Helene."

"Fine. Did he say who?"

"Nope."

IN SAN FRANCISCO, Pam Hale welcomed Barbara Grosvenor and her publicist, Hugh Gordon, to her television studio.

"I'm *so* sorry you've had all this trouble with your former husband," she said to Barbara, clasping her hand in both of her own.

"Thank you so much," Barbara said.

"I hope that what we do here today will go a long way

toward rectifying the situation." She handed Gordon a sheet of paper. "Please look this over and have Barbara sign it," Pam said.

Gordon scanned the sheet. "Minimum of half an hour," he muttered, "nonstop. That okay, Barbara?"

"Yes, of course."

"Wait a minute—no editing?"

"Oh, there'll be editing for time, but that's our professional responsibility," Pam said smoothly. "And, of course, we own the copyright."

"That's fine with me, Hugh," Barbara said. She took the document from him, signed it, and handed it back to Pam, who handed it to her producer. "Put that in your safe right now," she said to him, sotto voce.

They had made up a set to resemble a corner of a living room, with a vase of plastic flowers on a table between two wing chairs. An assistant wired up Barbara, and Pam settled her guest into a chair and put a bottle of water and a glass on the table for her, while an assistant took Hugh Gordon into the Green Room, where he could watch a monitor. "All ready?" Pam asked. "Comfortable?"

"Yes, thank you."

Pam got the signal through her earpiece, and she looked into one of the three cameras. "Hello, I'm Pamela Hale. My guest is Mrs. Charles Grosvenor—Barbara—who is one of San Francisco's leading socialites and a large contributor to many local arts programs." She turned to Barbara, and the director cut to a two-shot. "Barbara, you're talking with us today because, as you have put it, you have been subjected to a campaign of terror by your former husband, well-known attorney Ed Eagle, of Santa Fe."

"I'm afraid that's true, Pam. I wish it weren't, but that has been my lot for years now. Mr. Eagle has made repeated attempts on my life, then blamed me for them, and the police have been able to do nothing."

Pam took Barbara patiently through her allegations, drawing out all the pain and suffering she said she had been through, and doing more listening than talking. Barbara relaxed and let the venom pour from her lips in honeyed tones laced with sadness and regret.

Then, halfway through their half hour, Pam tacked onto a new course. "Barbara," she said, smiling, "I've been carefully through the public record of your life, and have interviewed others who've known you along the way, and there are some things in your background we need to address. Let's see, you were born the daughter of a pawnbroker in the Midwest, then moved to New York in your late teens. There you married a much older man, a diamond merchant." She looked inquiringly at Barbara for confirmation.

"Yes," Barbara said tentatively.

"Then, shortly after your marriage, you became involved with another man, a convicted felon with a history of violent crime, and with your help, he conducted a robbery of your husband's diamond business, during which he shot and killed your husband."

Barbara was looking nervously around for Hugh Gordon. "Well, that's a long story," she said.

"As a result, your lover was caught, tried, convicted, and

given a life sentence, and you were convicted of accessory to murder and sentenced to seven to ten years, is that correct?"

IN THE GREEN ROOM, Hugh Gordon, who had been half dozing, sat bolt upright in his chair. "What?" he yelled. But there was no one to hear him. He ran to the door, but it was locked, and hammering on it and shouting brought no response.

"IT WAS THERE, was it not, that you first met Ed Eagle, who came to interview you for information on another case. He took a liking to you and offered his help when you were released?"

"Yes, that was good of him," Barbara said.

"Then you obtained an early release from prison as a result of a court order aimed at ending prison overcrowding, and very shortly, you turned up in Santa Fe and renewed your acquaintance with Ed Eagle?"

"Yes," Barbara said.

"He gave you a job, and the two of you began to go out. Then, a few months later, you were married."

"The worst mistake of my life," Barbara said.

"Then, after a year or so of marriage, having gained your husband's trust, you emptied his bank and brokerage accounts and disappeared into Mexico." It wasn't a question.

"Well, you see, Ed had become very violent."

"Did you ever call the police?"

"No, I . . ."

"Did anyone else ever witness this violence?"

"I'm not sure."

"Did you have any visible injuries?"

"No, I . . ."

"Then, in Mexico, after being reunited with one of your sisters, who also had a criminal record, the two of you became involved with a young Mexican man in a sexual threesome, then you tortured the young man, mutilated him by cutting off his penis with a straight razor, and murdered him."

"That's an outrageous accusation!" Barbara nearly screamed.

"Perhaps so, but true," Pam said. "You were tried, convicted of murder, and sentenced to life in a Mexican prison, were you not?"

"It was a terrible miscarriage of justice."

"In prison, you formed a sexual liaison with the warden, did you not? Then you drugged him and escaped from a bathroom window in his apartment, and were met by an old friend from Los Angeles and spirited out of the country in a small airplane."

"It was the only way I could get away from being raped daily," Barbara said, rallying.

"After that you changed your identity and went to Los Angeles, where, one night, you entered a suite at the Bel-Air Hotel, where you believed Ed Eagle to be staying, and shot the occupant to death while he slept. You were arrested, then tried, and while you were waiting for the jury's verdict, you escaped from the courthouse and hid at a resort near Palm Springs, where you met your next husband, Mr. Grosvenor."

"I was acquitted!" Barbara shouted.

"Right, but you still had to plead to a charge of escaping from custody. After that, there was a series of attempts on the life of Ed Eagle, culminating in a knife attack by a killer you hired, which left Mr. Eagle in critical condition in a Santa Fe hospital."

"I had nothing to do with that!"

"Are you saying that Ed Eagle staged a nearly fatal knife attack on himself?"

"Of course he did. I'm not taking any more of this!" Barbara got to her feet and began ripping the wires from her body.

"Well, there's a great deal more here," Pam said, holding up her clipboard. "I guess I'll just have to continue without you."

The camera followed Barbara as she searched for a way out of the room, then Hugh Gordon appeared, breathless and red-faced. "This way!" he shouted, and the two of them made their escape from the studio.

Pam turned back to the camera. "In the absence of Mrs. Barbara Grosvenor, let's go through the rest of her history, which culminates with the explosion of Ed Eagle's jet airplane at Santa Monica Airport a few days ago."

Occasionally consulting her notes, Pam went on.

E veryone gathered in the early evening for a drink in Stone's living room. Hal Henry, an old Hollywood hand in his sixties, regaled them with stories of the town's golden years and held them rapt. Then Dino and Viv arrived with their guests, who turned out to be the police commissioner of New York and his wife, Dorothy. Stone knew them well, and was happy to see them. They were almost ready to go in for dinner, when Fred came into the room. "Telephone call for Ms. Keaton," he said.

"You can take it in the study," Stone said. She knew the way. Everyone chatted for a bit, then Ann returned. "Ed," she said, "you've gotten very lucky with *60 Minutes*: a segment they had planned to show this Sunday had to be held up while they sort out some legal problems and they were going to air a rerun, but the Pamela Hale interview from San Francisco came in and blew them away."

"That's wonderful news," Hal said. "You don't get on that show on short notice unless you have something special."

"They're doing a rough cut of the footage as we speak, and they want to come here tomorrow morning, show you the rough cut, then interview you on camera."

"Fine with me," Ed said.

"They're going to make two segments of the two interviews," Ann said. "The first segment will be softball questions from Pamela, allowing Barbara to get everything out of her system. That will be the interview her publicist wanted for her. The second segment will be taken from the last half of the interview, followed by the interview with you, Ed."

Hal Henry was nearly beside himself. "This is going to drive Hugh Gordon crazy. We've been rivals for years, and now all I have to do is find a way to take credit for the whole thing."

Everybody laughed. "I'll see if I can get you a credit," Ann said.

They went in to dinner, and the evening passed in good food, wine, and conversation. Stone reflected that he didn't give enough dinner parties, and he resolved to have more guests in his home.

When the dessert dishes were being taken away, the commissioner cleared his throat loudly. "Stone," he said, "may I have the floor for a moment?"

"Of course, Commissioner."

"I have a couple of announcements to make: we've been a long time coming to this final decision, but tomorrow morning, on the steps outside City Hall, I'm going to announce my candidacy for the Democratic nomination for mayor of New York City."

Applause from all.

"I had considered running as an independent, to avoid a crowded primary, but after consideration, and considering the quality of the field, we decided to enter. It will give us more airtime before the general election and, thus, an edge over the Republican candidate."

"That's great news, Commissioner," Stone said.

"There's a bit more," the commissioner said. "At the press conference, I'll also be announcing my resignation as commissioner, so that I can run full-time. Naturally, I have a great interest in who succeeds me, so today I had a meeting with the present mayor, also a good Democrat, and he has agreed to appoint Chief of Detectives Dino Bacchetti to the office of commissioner."

More applause.

"Dino has always been an outstanding cop, dating back to the days when he had Stone for a partner to keep him out of trouble, then as a sergeant and a lieutenant, when he led the detective squad at the Nineteenth Precinct. Although he has been chief of detectives for only a fairly short time, he has proved adept not only at leading the city's detectives, but in handling the more public side of the office. In short, he has been a big success as chief and my best appointment. And if

I'm elected and he keeps his nose clean, I'll reappoint him upon taking office."

Fred, without being asked, suddenly reappeared with a magnum of Dom Pérignon from Stone's cellar, and everyone drank to the old and new commissioners.

LATER, WHEN THE GUESTS had gone or retired, Stone and Ann made love until exhausted.

"I'm sorry I can't be here tomorrow to keep an eye on Ed's interview with Morley Safer," she said, "but that's the sort of thing Hal Henry does every day, and he'll see that Ed gets fair treatment."

"Don't worry about Ed," Stone said. "He's an old hand at this sort of thing, and the camera loves him."

"I'm not surprised," she replied. "Tomorrow, as I've said before, all hell breaks loose. I've got a meeting at eight A.M. where Kate's campaign schedule will be finalized, barring last-minute changes, then we look at our first television ads, which were shot in New York yesterday and today. I'm very nervous about those."

"The camera loves Kate, too," Stone said.

"The TV campaign will break the day after the Republican convention ends. If Henry Carson gets the nomination, as seems fairly certain, he won't have had time to get his TV campaign together, so we'll have several days for our ads to run unopposed, as it were. Also, Kate is doing two of the network morning shows tomorrow and two the day after, then she goes quiet with the beginning of the Republican convention until the ad campaign breaks."

"Sounds like you have everything under control," Stone said.

"It may sound that way, but things can change in an hour, sometimes in a minute, so I will always be reorganizing."

"No one does it better," Stone said.

She turned and reached for him again. "That's what I was just thinking about you."

S tone had an early breakfast at seven with Ann, who then dressed quickly and left for the campaign office. He read the *Times* and did the crossword, then dressed and got downstairs just in time to greet the *60 Minutes* crew. He showed them around the house while the Eagles and their party had breakfast in the kitchen, and the director chose Stone's study as his set for taping the interview.

He stopped by the kitchen before going to his office. "Everybody sleep well?" he asked.

There was a chorus of positive answers.

"They said they'd be ready for you, Ed, at eleven sharp in my study. Knock it out of the park."

"I'll do my best," Eagle said.

Stone went to his office and began returning phone calls and answering correspondence. Joan came in and turned on his TV. "Kate Lee's commercial was on just a minute ago," she said. "She's on *Morning Joe* right now, so I'll run it down for you." She went into the DVR and rewound. "Here we go."

Kate came on-screen in what appeared to be the study at the Carlyle apartment. "Hi," she said. "I'm Kate Lee, and you may have heard that I'm the Democratic nominee for president."

She continued talking conversationally, directing the viewer to her website for detailed policy information, while never breaking eye contact with the camera and not reading from a teleprompter. It was over in thirty seconds, leaving an impression of freshness, intelligence, and personal warmth.

"I'm convinced," Stone said. "She's got my vote."

"Yeah, but you're a pushover."

"How about you?"

"Well, I'm a pushover, too, I guess. And if I weren't, that ad would do it for me."

Eagle came in. "Got a minute?"

"Sure."

Ed dumped his long frame into a chair. "I just called Cessna, and I got lucky. They've got a Citation M2 coming off the line in a couple of weeks, and the buyer wants out. I can buy his position at a discount."

"And you need an airplane, as I recall."

"Yep. The insurance company has already seen what's left of the Mustang, and it's a total loss, so I get the hull value. The training course at FlightSafety in Wichita starts in a couple of weeks, too. You want to do it with me?"

"Why not? My airplane gets delivered the week after next. What's the course, two weeks?"

"That's it."

"You're on. Tell 'em to book me in the class with you, and I'll get Joan to book us a big two-bedroom suite at the airport hotel. Is Susannah coming?"

"Yes, she is. She's qualified to train for a copilot's rating, and she's looking forward to it."

"That's great, and when you get real old, you can swap seats."

Joan came in. "They're ready to show Ed the interview upstairs, then they'll record his riposte."

Ed disengaged from his chair and went upstairs.

BILLY BURNETT AWOKE early in his San Francisco hotel. After his trip to Napa he had found a room that faced the Grosvenor apartment, and he had a nice view from a block away and one floor above them, with about a thirty-degree angle. He raised the blinds and trained his binoculars on the apartment's terrace. The angle made it impossible to see into the living room, so he would just have to catch her outside. He had no idea what time she rose, so he would have breakfast facing her building and just wait to get sight of her.

BARBARA SLEPT PAST her usual early hour for rising, and when she awoke, she was still rattled by the course the interview had taken. Hugh Gordon had told her not to worry, that he would sit down with Pamela Hale and see that the editing went their way. He was going to try for having the whole second part of the interview cut, but he admitted that was a bit of a stretch.

She got out of bed as Charles emerged from his dressing room in a suit, ready for his day.

"Good morning, my darling," he said, offering a kiss on the forehead.

"Good morning," she said listlessly.

He took her by the shoulders. "Now, you're not still concerned about that interview, are you?"

"I'm still a little shaken," she said.

"Nothing a buck's fizz won't fix."

That was the British name for a mimosa, equal parts champagne and orange juice.

"Order me breakfast, will you? Just melon and coffee."

"And a buck's fizz?"

"Oh, all right, maybe it will help. I'll be right out."

BILLY HAD JUST finished his breakfast when a movement on the Grosvenors' terrace caught his eye. He trained the binoculars and saw a tall man in a good suit stride out onto the terrace. A maid came, handed him a newspaper, and spoke briefly with him.

Billy opened the briefcase containing the sniper's rifle that he had built for himself. He assembled it, then unscrewed the head of a fat golf umbrella and shook out the thirty-six-inch barrel that he had made for longer shots. It took only a moment to screw it in place. He rolled the room service tray table into the hallway, put the DO NOT DISTURB sign out, and locked the door. He pulled a chair from the desk to the window, set up a short tripod, then screwed the silencer into the barrel and sat down.

He had not quite got set up when Barbara appeared on the terrace in a dressing gown.

BARBARA TOOK HER seat opposite Charles, who looked up and smiled at her. For some reason, it annoyed her; he was always smiling at her or kissing her forehead or patting her ass in a proprietary way. She had found all this charming at first, but it had palled as the marriage wore on.

"Busy day today?" Charles asked.

"A board meeting and lunch at the museum," she said. "I may develop a cold, I haven't decided."

"How will they ever get on without you there?"

"How will they ever paper over the cracks in their budget without my checkbook at the ready? That's all they care about—certainly not my opinion."

BILLY USED THE telescopic sight, now. He checked a flag on top of her building and it hung slack. He got comfortable and set the rifle on the tripod. This was looking good.

He sighted, and discovered that at least three-quarters of

Barbara was behind her husband; he waited for one of them to move.

BARBARA FINISHED her melon. "I'm going to take my coffee and paper to bed," she said. "I'm more comfortable there." She got up and walked into the living room.

BILLY HAD NO more than an instant for a shot at her, but she was moving, and a sheet of newspaper on the table suddenly blew off with a puff of wind. Then she was inside, carrying her coffee and newspaper. He had missed his opportunity.

"Shit," he said aloud.

His cell phone began to ring, and he answered it. "This is Billy Burnett."

"Good morning, Billy, it's Peter. How are you feeling?"

"Much better, thank you, Peter."

"We've got that casting session you set up at three this afternoon. Will you be here for it?"

Billy had nearly forgotten. "Yes, Peter, I'll be there after lunch."

"See you then."

Billy hung up and began dismantling the rifle. This was going to have to wait, probably until after the weekend.

*C*harles Grosvenor arrived at the Bentley dealership, went directly to his office, and called Hugh Gordon, Barbara's newly hired publicist.

"Good morning, Charles," the man said smoothly.

"Hugh, how are you coming on the editing of Barbara's interview with that Hale woman?"

"Charles, I was going to call Barbara in a few minutes. I think I may have gotten the entire interview killed. The CEO at WSFO has told me that he has about decided not to run it."

"'About decided'? What does that mean?"

"It means he's seriously thinking about not running it. Pam is beside herself, of course, but it's her boss's decision, and he's leaning toward not running it."

"How can he be pushed all the way?"

"That's my job, Charles, and I'm working hard at it. I've

told the man that Barbara feels she was sandbagged, which she was, and that if the second part of the interview runs, she will consider legal action. He knows that Barbara has deep pockets and that a successful lawsuit could break his company, and I've also been feeding his concerns about the reaction of the arts community in San Francisco, which depends so heavily on Barbara for large contributions. I think he has begun to see that the consequences of running the interview are unpredictable, to say the least."

"Please be sure to convey all this directly to Barbara, Hugh. She's very upset, and frankly, she's driving me crazy. I need to get this business favorably settled and get her out of town. A change of scenery will do wonders for her."

"Is she awake now?"

"She is, and she would be grateful for your call."

"Then I'll call her as soon as we hang up. By the way, Charles, I'm interested in talking with you about a Bentley."

"Wonderful, Hugh. In which model does your interest lie?"

"The Flying Spur, I think."

"Hold on just a moment, will you, Hugh?"

"Certainly."

Charles pressed the hold button and checked his inventory on his computer, then he went back to the call. "Hugh, I have a new Flying Spur that's being used as a press car at the moment. Why don't you take it for the weekend and drive someplace beautiful? Down to Carmel or up to Napa?"

"I would be delighted," Hugh said.

"The car is its own best salesman," Charles said. "If you

have any questions, make a note of them. We'll have lunch early next week and I'll answer them."

"Wonderful, Charles."

"You can pick up the car here anytime Friday afternoon. Or, if you'd prefer, I'll have it delivered to you."

"I'll pick it up, I think."

"See you then."

Charles hung up feeling very much better. He could see an end to this interview business, and he had probably sold a car.

He called his service manager and instructed him to clean the car, and especially the upholstery. He wanted it to have that new-car smell when Hugh Gordon got into it.

He had to find a way to get Barbara happy again. He enjoyed being wealthy, and divorce would not be a good idea. He had seen the effect that rejection had on Barbara, and he did not wish to replace Ed Eagle as the object of her enmity.

STONE ACCEPTED AN invitation to lunch with Bill Eggers, the managing partner of his law firm, Woodman & Weld. They met at the Four Seasons, where Eggers had a regular table.

Eggers ordered his usual martini, and Stone had mineral water. He had found that it was important to have a clear head during these seemingly informal lunches with Bill.

"I'm sorry we didn't get to see more of you at the convention, Bill," Stone said. "It got rather busy."

"That's quite all right, Stone. All the insiders I know are giving you credit for swinging the nomination to Kate Lee."

"That's an exaggeration," Stone said.

"Still, it makes you an important FOK."

"A what?"

"Friend of Kate."

"Ah, yes."

"If she gets elected, of course. But right now, it looks like her election to lose. Have you seen her commercials?"

"Just one, on *Morning Joe*, earlier today."

"I think they're brilliant. Henry Carson, assuming he gets the Republican nomination, is going to look like the usual Republican stuffed shirt when compared to her. Hank makes Mitt Romney look like a hippie."

Stone laughed.

"And it doesn't hurt that half the men in America could imagine themselves in bed with Kate."

"Well, half the men you're acquainted with, Bill."

"Stone, as you know, we're thought of as a Democratic law firm, and we've been very close to Will Lee's administration."

"Yes, I know."

"I'd like us to be much closer to Kate's administration," Eggers said. "That's why I gave her super PAC a million dollars a while back. I assume that's why you did, too."

"No, that's not why. I just think she'd make a terrific president."

"That, too," Eggers said, smiling slightly. "Here's my advice, Stone—turn a section of your iPhone into a Rolodex of people close to Kate. It will become useful next year."

Stone couldn't disagree.

"And now that the convention is over, perhaps you could turn your attention to making some rain?"

"I'm always on the alert for new business, Bill. But remember, I have to go to Paris this fall for the opening of L'Arrington there."

Eggers groaned.

"What, isn't Marcel duBois a good enough client?"

"Well, now that you mention it, yes. Find me two or three more like him while you're over there."

"Bill, there *aren't* two or three more like Marcel."

"You know what I mean."

"Yes, Bill, I do."

51

When Stone got back from lunch, there was a note from Dino to be on the steps of City Hall at four o'clock. He buzzed Joan.

"Yes, my lord and master?"

"Find out how big a donation I can legally make to the mayoral campaign of Commissioner Tom Donnelly."

"Stone, were you drinking at lunch?"

"No, why?"

"The commissioner is not a candidate for mayor, to my knowledge."

"Your knowledge is out of date. He's announcing at four o'clock. Then the present mayor will appoint Dino police commissioner."

"Wow! I'll get right on it."

Stone hung up. A minute later Joan buzzed him.

"Yes?"

"Four thousand nine hundred and fifty dollars," she said.

"Are you sure that's all?"

"That's all."

"Okay, cut a check to Tom Donnelly for Mayor, put it in an envelope, and give it to me."

"Certainly."

Ed Eagle knocked on the inside door to Stone's office.

"Come in, Ed. Do you and Susannah want to go down to City Hall with me and watch Dino get sworn in as commissioner at four?"

"I'd love to," Ed said, "but Susannah is shopping, and I don't think I'd better disturb her."

"We'll have to leave shortly," Stone said. "Traffic's bad this time of day." He asked Joan to have Fred bring around the car.

THEY MADE IT to City Hall just in time; a crowd had already gathered on the steps. Stone and Ed got out of the car, and Fred moved off in search of parking.

Dino saw them and waved them around the crowd to where he stood with Viv. "You're in my party," he said. "Stand here."

Somebody tested the sound system, then the mayor stepped forward. "Ladies and gentlemen, it is my great honor to introduce Police Commissioner Tom Donnelly!" He stepped back and yielded the small podium, and the commissioner stepped forward.

"Good afternoon, everybody. I'm here to announce that I have just handed my resignation as police commissioner to the mayor, effective immediately, and that he has accepted it, I hope with regret." There was a chorus of nos, mixed with applause. "That said, I am here to announce my candidacy for mayor in the upcoming Democratic primary!" Much applause and cheering. The commissioner went on for another two minutes, listing some of the things he wanted to do. "And now, I believe the mayor has another announcement." He surrendered the podium.

"Actually," the mayor said, "I have two announcements. First, I think it would be a grave error to leave the position of police commissioner open, even for a day, and so I am very pleased to announce my appointment of Chief of Detectives Dino Bacchetti to the office of commissioner, effective immediately." Much applause, then the mayor continued. "Dino has served the NYPD at every level during a career that took him from patrolman, to detective, to lieutenant, to captain, and then to chief of detectives, in which office he has served brilliantly. And incidentally, Dino will be the youngest police commissioner of New York since Theodore Roosevelt, more than a hundred and twenty-five years ago! Dino, step up here and get sworn in."

Somebody produced a Bible, and Viv stepped forward to hold it.

"And holding the Bible," the mayor said, "is retired detective Vivian Bacchetti!"

Suddenly, there was a disturbance at the rear of the crowd. Stone, standing high on the steps, could see Fred Flicker's back as he fought someone else. He ran around the crowd, grabbing for his honorary badge, and approached a little knot of people. Fred was being pulled off a man who lay on his back on the steps, and a uniformed cop was relieving the man of a pistol. Two detectives, one of whom Stone knew, dragged Fred backward on his heels while one took Fred's gun from him.

Stone flashed his badge. "Hold on there, gentlemen," he said. "That man is with me, and he is licensed to carry that weapon. Show them your license, Fred."

Fred did so, and his gun was returned to him and holstered.

"What the hell is going on?" Stone asked one of the detectives.

"I'm not sure," the man said, "but I saw guns, and I got in there."

"Mr. Barrington," Fred said, "I saw that man draw a weapon and aim it, I think, at the mayor. I was the only person close to him, so I tackled him."

"Well done, Fred. You gentlemen, take him aside and get his ID and his statement. I'll be up there." He pointed to where Dino and the others stood, staring down at him, then he ran around the crowd and took up his former position behind Viv.

"May we continue now, Mr. Barrington?" the mayor asked.

"Yes, of course, sir. Someone was just trying to shoot you, but he was thwarted."

"Just as soon as I get Dino sworn in, I want to hear about that," the mayor said, and Stone nodded. The mayor returned to his work and took the oath from Dino—then he turned back to the crowd. "I have one more announcement to make," he said. "I am very pleased to offer my wholehearted, unconditional endorsement of Tom Donnelly as the next mayor of New York City!"

AFTERWARD, AS STONE was explaining to the mayor, Tom Donnelly, and Dino what had happened, he saw Fred leave the two detectives and approach. He waved the little man over. "Mayor," he said, "I'd like to introduce you to the gentleman who just saved your life. This is Frederick Flicker, formerly of the Royal Marines."

The mayor pumped Fred's hand, who looked embarrassed.

Fred shook the offered hands, then said, "I'd better get the car." And he did.

When they were driving uptown, Stone said, "Fred, I'm glad we got you that carry license."

"So am I, sir," Fred replied. "I considered shooting the man but thought better of it."

"I'm so glad you did, Fred," Stone said.

S tone waited dinner for Ann, and she managed to get home at eight o'clock, looking flustered.

"Anything bad happen?" Stone asked.

"That depends on your definition of 'bad,'" she replied, then she threw up her hands. "Don't ask!"

"All right, I won't." He led her to the study and poured her a martini. "Helene is putting the finishing touches on dinner," he said.

"So, how was your day?"

"Well, let's see. The police commissioner resigned from office and announced for mayor. The mayor appointed Dino to succeed as commissioner, effective immediately, and Fred tackled a gunman and saved the mayor's life."

"*What?* Tell me everything!"

Stone told her everything. He was about to pour them another drink when Fred entered the study.

"Excuse me, Mr. Barrington, dinner is served in the kitchen."

"Fred," Ann said, "I want to congratulate you on your bravery this afternoon. I've heard all about it, and that was a marvelous piece of work."

"Thank you, ma'am," Fred said. "I saw my duty, and I done it, that's all."

"That's all anyone can ask of a man," Stone observed.

"Ah, Mr. Barrington, I'm sorry to bring this up, but I've been besieged by all sorts of newspaper and television people for interviews."

"Do you want to become even more famous, Fred? If so, grant the interviews."

"Oh, no, sir, I was trained to do my duty quietly and avoid public exposure."

"Then ask Joan to tell them all that Mr. Flicker wishes to maintain his privacy and not grant any interviews or photos."

"A very good plan, Mr. Barrington. I'll tell Joan."

Fred led them downstairs as if they didn't know the way and seated Ann while Stone selected a bottle from the wine cooler. He decanted it and poured them each a glass.

"Oh, Greek food!" Ann enthused. "My favorite."

"Now that Helene has heard you say that, you may never be given anything else," Stone said.

They dined on dolmades—stuffed vine leaves—and moussaka—a casserole of lamb and aubergines covered with a béchamel sauce—and drank the sturdy Amarone Stone had chosen. Stone shooed Helene and Fred out of the kitchen, telling them to worry about the dishes tomorrow.

IN LOS ANGELES, Billy and Betsy Burnett were leaving the studio together for the drive home.

"What happened in San Francisco?" Betsy asked.

"Oh, nothing," Billy replied.

"Come on, Billy, do you think I don't know why you went there for two nights?"

"Don't make suppositions."

"I'm not supposing, I *know*. And if you've resumed killing people, then I think I have a right to know so that I can help keep anyone from finding out. You'll need an alibi, you know."

"Darling," Billy said, "I promise I will never put you in such a position that you will need to give me an alibi."

"*What happened in San Francisco?*" she demanded.

"When I said nothing, I was telling the truth."

"Billy, when you undertake something like that, *something* happens."

"It's not that I didn't try," Billy said, sighing. "I made two attempts, both foiled by circumstances."

"Oh, I'm so glad," Betsy said.

"Don't be glad—it will have to be done at some point."

"Will it really, Billy? Isn't there another way?"

"Ed Eagle has been trying every other way for years, to no avail. It's down to me, now. I'm all he has left."

"Well, I can't tell you not to get involved, I guess. Ed is a friend of Stone's, and we owe Stone so much."

"I was able to pass something on to Stone that I hope will help. Barbara is starting a campaign of interviews to make Ed look like the bad guy in all this."

"That's terrible!"

"Yes, and I hope that someone can do something to counteract her campaign."

"Don't worry yourself, Stone will think of something."

"I hope you're right," Billy said. "Otherwise, I'm going to have to think of something else. Barbara and her husband are looking for a house in Bel-Air, I hear. If they find something in L.A., that will make her more accessible."

"I just hope this all goes away," Betsy said.

"It will go away," Billy replied. "One way or another."

ANN PUT HER fork down. "That was just *wonderful*," she said. "Now I think I have the fortitude to tell you what happened today."

"That sounds bad."

"As I said before, it depends on how you define 'bad.'"

"Tell me."

"You must never breathe a word of this to a living soul," she said. "Promise?"

"I promise."

Ann took a deep breath. "I think Kate may be pregnant."

S tone sat and stared at Ann. "Did Kate tell you that?"

"No, she didn't, but you know how cool and calm Kate always is?"

"Yes, I've noticed that about her."

"Well, now she's nervous to the point where she's been throwing up. I've caught her twice."

"I should think that being the candidate is enough to make her nervous."

"Maybe, but have you seen any of the campaign commercials?"

"Only one."

"Did you notice how she seemed to . . . *glow*?"

"That was probably just makeup."

"She wasn't wearing makeup," Ann said. "The director told her she didn't need it. Only two things make a woman glow like that—a new love or pregnancy."

"I wouldn't think there would be time in her life for a new love."

"No, there wouldn't be, and she loves Will Lee so intensely that it just wouldn't be possible."

"So, to your mind, the only other possibility is . . ."

"Exactly."

"Let me ask you this: If she were pregnant, do you think she would tell you?"

"I've thought about that, and I believe she would. I don't think she would tell Molly, they don't have that kind of relationship—but Kate and I do."

"Would she tell Will?"

"Oh, yes, she wouldn't keep that from him."

"How old is Kate?"

"That's classified," Ann said, "and you will never have a high enough security clearance to find out."

"All right, is she fifty yet?"

"I'll give you that much—no."

"Has she been through menopause?"

"No. I would know about that."

"Then it's possible she could be pregnant."

"It's extremely unlikely. I mean, she has the son, Peter, from her first marriage to Simon Rule, but that was a long time ago. I happen to know that she and Will have one hell of a good sex life—that's classified, too—but I always thought Will might be sterile. On the other hand, she could have been on the pill all that time."

"Well, it would certainly be a first," Stone said. "A pregnant presidential candidate."

"The first that we know about," Ann said.

"Have you thought about the ramifications?"

"I've thought of nothing else all day. All week, really, but my suspicion has been growing."

"Are you going to ask her?"

"Certainly not—that would limit her options."

"How do you mean, options?"

"Well, she could choose to have an abortion," Ann said. "She's strongly pro-choice, and I assume for herself as much as for other women."

"If she decided to do that, do you think she would reveal it—either before or after the fact?"

"Certainly not before the fact, but after, who knows? I mean, there are more people in this country who favor a woman having the option, if polls are to be believed."

"And most of those who are opposed to it would be opposed to Kate anyway, wouldn't they?"

"Among Republicans, yes. Among independents, maybe. It's not a political calculation I'd want to have to make."

"Then suppose she decides to have the baby? That would pose wardrobe problems, wouldn't it?"

"I don't think so. After all, Kate is tall and slim, and she told me once that when she was pregnant with Peter, she hardly showed at all. She was an analyst at the Agency then, and she wasn't sure how her superiors would react, since they were all men at that time."

"Then she might be able to keep a pregnancy secret, until after the election?"

"Conceivably," Ann said, "pun intended."

"All right, suppose she announced it, or that the news leaked? What effect would it have on the campaign?"

"I believe," Ann said, "not to put too fine a point on it, it would cause the biggest fucking uproar you could possibly imagine. Think of the royal baby, and multiply that by a hundred."

"What kind of uproar? Favorable or unfavorable?"

"Your guess is as good as mine. It's the sort of thing we'd need to do a poll on, and we certainly can't do that."

"What about the opinion of women?"

"My guess would be, supportive, at least most women."

"And men?"

"Horrified. But maybe I'm wrong, who knows?"

"What are you going to do, Ann?"

"I'm going to wait until Kate decides to tell me."

"And what will you do then?"

"Punt."

S tone called Dino.

"Commissioner's office," a gruff male voice said.

"This is Stone Barrington. May I speak to the commissioner, please?"

"Who?"

"He'll know the name."

"Tell me again."

"Stone . . . Barrington. Would you like me to spell it?" He was put on hold without comment.

After a count of about forty, the voice came back. "Commissioner," he said, "the Barrington guy is on."

"Stone?" Dino said.

"I think so," Stone replied. "After talking with your new secretary, I'm not sure."

"Oh, that guy. Tom liked an all-male presence on the phones. He thought it sounded more official."

"You need some women in there, pal. What happened to your old secretary?"

"I had to leave her behind to break in the new chief of detectives."

"So who's the new chief?"

"I haven't decided. There are several candidates."

"Want some free advice?"

"What's it going to cost me?"

"Nothing, if you follow it. Appoint a woman."

"Are you kidding me? You think all those squad guys out in the precincts would take orders from a woman?"

"Think of it this way: Could Viv do the job?"

"Hah!" Dino snorted. "She could do *this* job, and probably better than I can."

"There's your answer."

"Appoint Viv? I can't do that."

"If Viv is good enough to do the job, there are other women around there who can do it, too. How many women in the department are captains?"

"I don't know, half a dozen, maybe eight."

"There's your short list. How many of them had a career as a detective?"

"Probably most of them."

"Here's what you do—call your old secretary and have her look up all their files and e-mail them to you. Don't tell anybody anything. If some of them look good for it, interview them. But not in your office. Somewhere else."

"Where could I interview them? I can't take them to the restaurants around here."

"Have them up to your apartment and interview them there. And don't forget to tell Viv what you're doing."

"What am I going to do about the four guys camped outside my office, answering the phones and typing letters?"

"Are they all sergeants?"

"Yeah."

"Get them out of there. Give them plum jobs in different precincts. And tell them that if they pass the lieutenant's exam, you'll promote them. They won't have anything to bitch about."

"I've got a public affairs guy I like. Should I replace him with a woman?"

"If you like him, keep him. If he's a sergeant, promote him, too."

"He's already a lieutenant."

"Then tell him to take the captain's exam. The rank will give him more authority with the press."

"You think I should have four women outside my door?"

"If you do, three of them should be in uniform. And the hell with the new chief—get your old secretary up there. If the new guy's any good, he'll find his way. You did."

"Tom should have appointed *you* commissioner," Dino said.

"Horseshit. Can you and Viv get free for dinner? Just me, Ann's working."

"Viv's on the road again. I can make it at eight. Patroon?"

"See you there." Stone hung up and found Ed Eagle standing in the doorway.

"You off?"

"Just waiting for Fred to bring the car around," Eagle said, sitting down.

"When's your plane?"

"In two hours."

"You'd better tell Fred to shake his ass."

"That's plenty of time, Stone."

"How long since you flew commercial?"

"Inside the U.S.? I can't remember the last time."

"You need to be there very early these days, so they can strip you and do a cavity search."

Eagle laughed. "It's that bad, is it?"

"Just don't smart off to one of those ladies with the little wand, when she waves it at your crotch."

"I'll keep my mouth shut."

"They'll probably want to examine your dental work, too."

"I'll open up on request."

"And tell me you aren't armed or carrying anything in your briefcase."

"It's in my bag," Ed said.

"Loaded?"

"Unloaded."

"Where's the ammunition?"

"In the bag."

"Put it in another bag, not the same one with the gun."

"Oops, I'd better do that now."

"You'd better tell Susannah, too."

"Tell me what?" Susannah asked from the doorway.

"Not to go into the terminal armed."

Eagle explained it to her.

"Okay, I'll do some repacking, too."

"Do it now," Stone said, "not at the terminal. And remember to declare the weapons at the ticket desk. There's a form you have to fill out."

"All right, all right," Eagle said, getting up. "I'll tell Fred to open the trunk." They said their goodbyes and left by the street exit.

Stone got to Patroon first; the owner, Ken Aretzky, had already settled him in a booth with a drink, when he heard half the patrons burst into applause, and looked up to see Dino arriving, blushing and waving at the crowd.

"Commissioner," Ken said, "congratulations. It's an honor to have you here."

Dino leaned in close. "Thanks, Ken, now go fuck yourself."

Aretzky walked away laughing and signaled a waiter to bring Dino a drink.

"Can you believe all that?" Dino asked, sliding into a booth.

"You'd better get used to it, pal, it's going to be that way until you retire or get thrown out."

A bottle of wine they hadn't ordered arrived, and it was an expensive one.

"Jesus, I can't take that," Dino said.

"We'll pretend it's for me," Stone said. "Perfect," he said to the waiter. "I'll taste it."

The waiter poured him some, and Stone sampled it. "We'll drink it," he said, and the waiter poured for both of them.

Dino tried it. "That's the best bottle of wine I've ever had, outside your house," he said.

"So," Stone said, "how was your first day?"

"Well, I got Maxie back."

"Who?"

"My secretary, Maxie."

"I never knew that was her name."

"It's Maxine, but she hates that. And she got me the files on the lady captains, too."

"Have you had a chance to look them over?"

"I did, and I realized there is one outstanding choice—Stephanie Walters."

"The new captain at the one-niner?"

"New two years ago," Dino said. "As a detective, she had a better arrest record than I did, and she's known to be squeaky clean. She made captain a lot sooner than I did, too."

"That's only because you wouldn't take the exam until Tom Donnelly made you."

"Maybe."

"Are you going to interview her?"

"I got her down to my office this afternoon and offered her the job, and she took it in a flash."

"What sort of family has she got?"

"An ex-husband, who's captain at the four-four, in Brooklyn.

Two kids—a boy in his first year of law school at John Jay, and a girl who's a senior at Harvard Law. The girl wants to be an ADA, and the boy's headed for the department. Their grandfather was commissioner, back in the day."

"She sounds perfect."

"A looker, too, a redhead. The press loves her. Listen, pal, I've got to thank you—if not for our conversation this morning, I wouldn't have even thought of her."

"Don't mention it."

"I've scattered my sergeants to the four winds, and Stephanie had recommendations for three female sergeants, who'll be at their desks on Monday."

"Is everybody happy?"

"I promoted all the old sergeants to detective. Believe me, they're happy."

"Sounds like you had a good day."

"I did, I did. How was yours?"

"I saw off Ed and Susannah this morning. Can you believe they didn't know the rules for carrying guns on the airline? They haven't flown commercial in years."

"If you hadn't told them, I'd be getting them out of jail about now," Dino said. "How's Ann's job going since Kate got the nomination?"

"She's pretty busy," Stone said.

"Hey, I had a funny thought this afternoon, apropos of nothing. What would happen if Kate got pregnant?"

Stone choked on his drink.

"Not a good idea to inhale bourbon," Dino said. "Did I strike a nerve?"

Stone gradually got control of himself. "Don't ever say that," he said.

"Say what? If Kate got pregnant?"

"Shut up, Dino," Stone whispered "There are half a dozen media types within spitting distance of us, and waiters are nosy, too. If you were overheard saying that, the press would have her with child by morning. That's how rumors start."

"You mean she's *not* pregnant?"

"Well, she hasn't intimated any such thing to me," Stone said.

"Can you imagine the uproar if she was?"

"Just barely. Now stop talking about that. Tell me who you're going to fire, now that you have the power."

"Oh, there are a few guys who've been on the job longer than is good for the department," Dino said. "I'll find ways to ease them out."

"You crafty bastard! I'm glad you weren't commissioner when *I* was a cop!"

S tone got home to find Ann sitting naked in bed, watching the Republican convention. Stone got naked and joined her. "I'd forgotten it was on," he said.

"They're balloting, and Henry Carson is well ahead. No excitement here."

They watched listlessly while the balloting continued, and the TV guys gave the nomination to Carson. So did the convention, a short time later.

"Tell me about Carson," Stone said.

"Somebody said he makes Mitt Romney look like a hippie. Is that enough?"

"Is he smart?"

"About as smart as the average Republican senator."

"Is he a veteran?"

"Yes, of what, in his day, was called the draft-dodger program of the Air National Guard. He flew tankers. Around the Southwest."

"Well, at least he's a pilot."

"Yeah, he is—flies his own airplane, like you, except it's not a jet, it's a little one."

"What kind?"

"I don't know."

"How long has he been in the Senate?"

"Four terms. He'll be up for reelection in two years if he doesn't win the election."

"Who's his VP nominee going to be?"

"Probably Max Post, of Texas, whose sobriquet is 'Thick as a post Post.'"

"Is he the guy who suggested that Texas should secede from the Union?"

"One of them."

"You think we should let them?"

"In my heart, yes, but the good news is that the Hispanic population there is growing so fast that the Republicans soon won't be able to elect a candidate to statewide office."

"Has Kate told you whether she's pregnant, yet?"

Ann clasped her belly. "Oh, God, every time I hear that word my stomach does a backflip. Soon, I'll be having morning sickness myself."

"You're not . . ."

"Of course not. I have been a religious observer of the

pill-a-day routine." She looked at him slyly. "What would you do if I were pregnant?"

"What could I do? I'd be helpless."

She laughed.

"Are you worried about your biological clock?"

"I never consult it," she replied. "I gave up the thought of having a family when Kate got the nomination. By the time she's out of office I'll be withered and sere."

"You're sure about that?"

"Absolutely. I was born without the mother gene. I'm a working girl, through and through."

"Dino's appointing a woman chief of detectives."

"Good for Dino! Who is she?"

"Her name is Stephanie Walters, she's captain at Dino's and my old precinct, the Nineteenth. A ravishing redhead, divorced, mother of two, both in law school, one at Harvard, twenty-two years on the force."

"That's a pretty good résumé," Ann said. "Does she have a law degree?"

"I believe so."

"Maybe I'll suggest her for head of the FBI, or something."

"I think she's worth keeping track of."

"Don't worry, her name is already etched on my frontal lobe."

Stone turned off the TV. "Listen, as long as we're both naked . . ."

"You, too? I hadn't noticed."

He snuggled up to her. "Notice that?"

"Hard to miss," she said, turning over and embracing him.

———

HALF AN HOUR later, she said, "Did I tell you Ed is a go on *60 Minutes* Sunday night?"

"I had assumed he was."

"Morley Safer loved Ed. I have that from the horse's mouth."

"And it doesn't hurt that he's married to Susannah Wilde?"

"Not a bit."

"You know what Dino said to me at dinner?"

"What?"

"He said, out of the blue, 'What would happen if Kate got pregnant?'"

"Oh, God, does he know something?"

"Nothing—he just said it. I had to shut him up before a waiter overheard him and passed it to some gossip columnist across the dining room."

"You think Dino has a sixth sense about things?"

"Only about who committed a homicide."

"Pretty soon I've got to ask her," Ann said. "I can't stand it much longer."

57

S aturday afternoon Ann was in her office at the New York campaign headquarters. Henry Carson had made his acceptance speech as presidential nominee of the Republican Party, and had chosen the Texan, Max Post, as his running mate.

Outside, it was a blustery New York day that had a touch of autumn in it. Kate Lee was out making campaign appearances in New Jersey and, later, Long Island. Will Lee was holed up at the Carlyle apartment doing, apparently, not much of anything.

The phone rang, and Ann picked it up. "Ann Keaton."

"Hi there, it's Kate," a cheerful voice said.

"Good morning. How's it going in New Jersey?"

"Everyone has been just wonderful out here," Kate replied. "I've only got a second. I want you to do something for me."

"Anything."

"Set up a press conference for tomorrow morning at nine o'clock sharp. I want it in a small theater, like the one at the Museum of Modern Art—no more than five hundred seats, smaller if possible. Bill it as a major press conference, okay? And tell Jim I want that cell phone blocker thing."

"Okay. What's the subject?"

But Kate had already hung up. Ann made some calls: the MoMA auditorium wasn't available, but she came up with an ideal venue on East Sixtieth Street. She typed up the release and took it to the press secretary, who sat next door to her.

He looked at the release. "What's this about?" he asked. "Nobody consulted me."

"I don't know. She just called and instructed me to do that. And she wants the cell phone blocker."

"I'm going to call her and find out what's going on. I don't like being kept in the dark."

"Jim," she said, "you're aware that I know Kate a lot better than you do, right?"

"Yeah, sure."

"Then trust me when I tell you that she's not going to like it if her cell starts ringing for what she considers no reason. Put out the release. And if anybody asks you what it's about, tell them you're not going to tell them. That will ensure added interest. Everybody will be there because they'll be afraid they'll miss something important if they aren't."

"Whatever you say, Ann." He started typing the e-mail.

Ann went back to her desk feeling a little queasy. Nine o'clock on a Sunday morning was a strange time to call a press conference. The P word raised its ugly head. Ann knew Kate well enough that she wouldn't call a press conference to announce something like that. What she would call a press conference for was to announce that she was pregnant and leaving the race. Ann knew she wouldn't be seeing Kate tonight, so she wouldn't have an opportunity to talk her out of it.

She thought about it for a while and decided there was one other person who might know what was going on. She made the call to Governor Richard Collins's cell phone.

"Dick Collins."

"Dick, it's Ann Keaton. How are you?"

"I'm just great, getting ready to make a speech in Vermont to a convention of the Benevolent Order of the Moose. I'm not staying for the luncheon because I'm afraid of what they might be serving."

"I can't blame you. Listen, tell me what the press conference tomorrow morning is about."

"I have a press conference on a Sunday morning?"

"Not you, Kate. Surely she's talked with you about it."

"Not a word," Collins replied. "That's funny, she sends us a daily schedule, and there's nothing on it for tomorrow morning. What time?"

"Nine A.M."

"At a church?"

"No, she asked for a small auditorium in New York. She's in New Jersey and Long Island today."

"That is odd," he said. "Should I call her and ask about it?"

"I have a feeling that if she hasn't told you about it, she

doesn't want you to know. The only reason she told me is that somebody had to find an auditorium and put out a release."

Collins was silent for a long moment. "Ann," he said, "if Kate had decided to drop out of the race for some reason, she would have given me a heads-up, wouldn't she?"

"Sure she would, Dick," Ann half lied. "And listen, don't tell anybody about this—only you, me, and Jim Marks, our press secretary, know about it. Something's up, I'll grant you, but Kate clearly doesn't want anyone to know what."

"I understand."

"So please don't start trying to line up support for the nomination, just in case. If she doesn't drop out, you'd look like an ass."

"I get the picture, Ann. Let me know if there are further developments, will you?"

"I will let you know if there are further developments." Ann hung up.

There were no further developments.

58

Stone was very hungry by the time Ann got home. She came into the study and kissed him, then flopped on the sofa next to him.

"I thought we'd order a pizza," he said.

"Fine."

"The usual?"

"Fine."

Stone made the call.

"What's wrong?" he asked.

"Nothing."

"Something is clearly wrong. I've never seen you so clenched before."

"That doesn't mean something's wrong," she said.

"Then what does it mean?"

"It means that if something *is* wrong, I don't know what it is."

"I thought you knew everything. Why don't you know?"

"Because she won't tell me."

"Who won't tell you?"

"Kate."

"Kate thinks there's something wrong, but she won't tell *you*?"

"Exactly. I think so anyway."

"Ann, are you developing a paranoid streak?"

"I've always had a paranoid streak," she said. "I just won't admit it."

"But you just did."

"Then take that as a compliment. You are now the only one who knows. Besides my father and mother, of course. And a few college friends. And Kate."

"But besides all of them, I'm the only one who knows?"

"Right."

"I'll take that as a compliment. Is there any way I can help you figure this out?"

"No. You know even less than I do about what's wrong."

"When did you first get the feeling that something was wrong?"

"When Kate called me and asked me to call a press conference for tomorrow morning at nine."

"On a Sunday morning?"

"Yes."

"Something's wrong," he said.

"I knew it!" she shouted, leaping to her feet. "You've just confirmed it!"

"But I don't know anything."

"Welcome to the club! You see how it feels?"

"I'm beginning to," he admitted. "I'm beginning to think that paranoia is contagious."

"Maybe so. I'm starving. When is the pizza coming?"

"It won't be long, they're right around the corner." The doorbell rang; Stone ran to the front door and came back with a pizza. He got a bottle of wine from the cooler in the bar, opened it, and came back with two glasses and some napkins.

Ann had already dug into the pizza and was halfway through her first slice. She made a grateful noise when he handed her a glass of wine, then took a huge gulp. "Better," she said.

THE FOLLOWING MORNING Stone and Ann had an early breakfast. She kept looking at her watch.

"What time do you want to be there?" he asked.

"Eight-thirty," Ann said. "There's nothing for me to do until then. The press secretary is dealing with the lighting and sound system."

"I want to come with you," Stone said.

"Okay."

"You think she's pregnant?" he asked.

"No, but I don't know anything anymore. If she is pregnant, then she'll be leaving the race."

"Really?"

"No, not really, that's just my best guess."

"Have you ever noticed that when the president or somebody important has a press conference, everybody in the media already knows what it's about before it starts? I mean, they're telling you on TV what it's going to be about and what questions are going to be asked and what the answers will be."

"I've noticed that," Ann said. "It's because people like me leak it to a few people to guarantee good coverage and, if it's bad news, to soften the blow."

"It's a strange business," Stone said.

"What's strange is what's happening today," Ann said. "Nobody knows anything except Kate—and Will. Maybe."

THEY WERE IN the steeply raked little auditorium and in their seats at precisely eight-thirty. Members of the press, festooned with ID badges, were filing into the rows, and a gang of photographers sat on the floor between the first row of seats and the podium, keeping low enough not to be seen on TV.

"This is exciting," Stone said.

"Are you out of your fucking mind?" Ann asked. "It's terrifying!"

"I'll bet you're one of those people who reads the last couple of pages in a mystery novel before you start the book."

"How did you know that?" she demanded.

"It's clear you have no tolerance for suspense."

"But you're enjoying it?"

"I'm enjoying not knowing," Stone said. "You should try it sometime, it's fun."

"This is not a mystery novel," she said. "This is the future of the country and the planet."

"Oh, come on. Dick Collins will make a fine president if Kate decides not to run."

"Don't say those last words," Ann said. "Hearing them is like having my throat cut."

"Look on the bright side—if she doesn't run, you can come to Paris with me. We'll have a wonderful time—then when we come back, you can accept a job at Woodman and Weld, and we'll have a nice life."

"A nice life is the worst possible thing that could happen to me right now," she said. "I want a crazy, unpredictable, demanding, untamable life for the next eight years."

"I watched a documentary the other day about White House chiefs of staffs. I didn't want to tell you this, but do you know what the average tenure of the last forty chiefs of staff was?"

"I don't know, a couple or three years?"

"Less than a year and a half," Stone said.

"You're kidding me."

"I kid you not. They burn out fast—the stress is too much."

"I want the stress!" Ann said. "I want it all. I want it for eight years!"

"Not going to happen," Stone said. "What makes you think you could take it any better than any of the last forty in that job?"

"I'm smarter and tougher than they are," Ann said.

"I believe you, but when you burn the candle at both ends, the light doesn't last long."

Suddenly the lights in the room went off, and there was a sudden hush. Then the stage lights came up and Kate Lee strode to the podium.

She looked wonderful, Stone thought. She was wearing a beautiful silk dress that flowed when she walked and, yes, she was glowing.

"Good morning, everybody," Kate said as if she had invited them all to a garden party. "I have some wonderful news, but before I tell you I want you to know that the doors are locked, and your cell phones won't work in here, and I'm going to take only three questions when I'm done. Then, when I've made my escape, the doors will be unlocked."

That created a buzz.

Kate took a deep breath. "I am delighted to tell you that my husband and I are going to have a baby, and it's due next May."

There was a noise from the crowd that Stone had never heard before: equal parts of shock, outrage, and delight.

"First question," Kate said, pointing at a woman in the first row.

"Are you dropping out of the race?" she asked.

"Certainly not," Kate replied. "There are tens of thousands of working women all across this country who are having babies, then mixing motherhood and work, and some of them are top executives in large companies. If I quit, it would be an insult to every working mother." She pointed to a man in the middle of the group. "Second question."

"How are you going to take care of a baby and run the country at the same time?" he asked.

"I will have a secret weapon," Kate said, turning to her right and pointing. Will Lee had just appeared at stage right. "It's called a house husband. Ladies and gentlemen, meet Mr. Mom!"

There was a roar of laughter and applause, and Will was smiling.

"That man has never even *seen* a diaper," Kate said, "but God bless him, he has signed on for the duration." She pointed to a woman in the back row. "Third and final question."

"Who knows about this?" the woman asked.

"Not a soul in the world," Kate said, "except the people in this room. And when I walked in here, only one of those knew." Will walked over, kissed her, took her hand, and they walked off the stage.

The crowd of reporters rushed up the aisles, and a moment later, a hammering could be heard as they banged on the doors. Many people stood around, trying to get their cell phones to work. Then, the doors opened, and they flooded out of the room, up the stairs, and out the doors.

Ann had not stood up until now. "Wow!" she said, her hand on her chest. "I have never felt this good in my whole life!"

THEY WENT HOME and turned on the TV to the morning political shows. Every one of them showed the full tape of Kate's news conference, and every one of them had a table full of commentators talking about it. Toward the end of each show, Henry Carson was interviewed.

"Now I see why Kate did it on Sunday morning," Ann said. "Carson was the headliner on every show, and she blew him right out of the water. Nobody will ever remember what he said! And tomorrow morning, Kate will have the headline in every newspaper, and Carson will be buried inside!"

59

*O*n Sunday evening, Stone and Ann settled in to watch *60 Minutes.* "I didn't see any promos for this," Stone said.

"That's because it's a secret," Ann replied. "They didn't want Barbara Grosvenor to know about it, because she would probably have tried for a court injunction to block it."

The front-end teaser on the show was simple. Morley Safer looked into the camera and said, "Tonight, we have something different for you. Everybody knows someone who went through the divorce from hell, but this one adds something extra— repeated attempted murder. Stay tuned for the fireworks."

"That's the first time I've seen this show open without excerpts from the interviews."

"Great hook, wasn't it?"

CUT AND THRUST

IN LOS ANGELES, Billy and Betsy Burnett watched the show. "Uh-oh," Billy said, "I think I know who this is."

"This is what you were talking about, isn't it?" Betsy asked. "Barbara's PR campaign to destroy Ed Eagle?"

"I'm afraid so."

IN SAN FRANCISCO, Charles Grosvenor was watching the evening news at his desk at the dealership. He was there to receive the Bentley he had loaned Hugh Gordon, and Gordon had just driven up. He came into the office just as *60 Minutes* began, and he heard Morley Safer's opening remark.

"What the hell?" he said.

"This isn't about Barbara, is it?" Charles asked.

"It can't be. The station manager told me he wasn't . . ." He stopped and thought.

"He wasn't what?"

"That he wasn't going to run the interview. He didn't tell me that *60 Minutes* was going to run it."

"Oh, shit," Charles said. He grabbed the phone and called home; the number was busy. He tried Barbara's cell phone, but it went directly to voice mail. "Sweetheart," he said, "call me immediately!" He hung up just as Safer returned.

"Some years ago," Safer was saying, "a prominent trial attorney from Santa Fe married a woman called Barbara. He says now that it turned out to be the worst mistake he ever

295

made. Our correspondent Pamela Hale interviewed Barbara Eagle, now Mrs. Charles Grosvenor, and got her side of the story."

Charles tried the number again; still busy. "I've got to get home," he said. "There's no telling what she'll do if she sees this." He let himself and Hugh Gordon out of the building and locked it behind them.

"I'm awfully sorry about this, Charles," Gordon said. "I did everything I could to prevent it."

"My advice to you, Hugh, is get out of town—take a vacation," Charles said. "Maybe in a couple of weeks she'll have cooled off." He got into his car and drove away. Traffic was bad: people coming back from their weekends.

STONE AND ANN watched the first part of the interview. "That was awful," Ann said. "If she'd gotten away with that, Ed would be ruined."

"We haven't seen the next part," Stone replied. "Ed may be ruined yet."

Part two came on, and they watched, transfixed, as Pamela Hale backed Barbara into a corner, allegation by allegation, until Barbara fled the set, tripping over her microphone wire.

"I've never seen anything like that on television," Stone said. "Hale just burned her down."

Then Safer came back on and introduced Ed Eagle. "Ed," he said, "you've just watched Barbara's interview. What did you think of it?"

"I was absolutely stunned, Morley. It was like reading a false biography, written by your worst enemy."

"Let's go back to the beginning of this relationship," Safer said. "How did you first meet Barbara?"

"I visited a women's prison in upstate New York, where I had arranged to interview Barbara for some background on an upcoming trial. She made a very big impression on me."

"A favorable impression?"

"Oh, yes. As you saw in the first part of her interview, Barbara can be a charming and fascinating person to talk with. I asked her to come and see me in Santa Fe when she got out and told her that I'd help her restart her life. She had another four or five years to serve."

"But she got out sooner, didn't she?"

"Yes. The State of New York, under a court order, was required to alleviate overcrowding in their prisons, and they adopted an early-release program. Barbara managed to qualify for it, and she turned up in Santa Fe a few weeks after our first meeting."

With Safer leading the way, Eagle went on to recount the high and low points of their marriage.

When they were done, Stone switched off the TV. "He did it!" he said. "He made up the lost ground and then some!"

"With a lot of help from Barbara," Ann pointed out.

CHARLES GROSVENOR KEPT trying his home number as he drove, and finally Barbara answered.

60

B arbara picked up the phone. "Yes?"

"It's Charles," he said.

"Get home!" she said. "And right now!"

"What's wrong, dearest?"

"Disaster! Catastrophe! Why did I let myself get talked into doing that interview?" Her voice was pitched higher than usual, and it wavered. "Hugh Gordon is going to pay for this."

"Oh, come now, it can't have been all that bad."

"That woman knew everything, and I mean everything! She knew about Mexico, for God's sake. How could she know about that?"

"Now, Barbara," Charles said soothingly, "you've got to get ahold of yourself."

"Order the airplane!" she shouted. "We're leaving the country tonight!"

"Where shall I tell them to take us, sweetheart?"

"Anywhere they can't get at me."

"London, then?"

"Yes, London. Call the pilot right now, then come home and pack."

"I'll get right on it, my dear." Charles hung up.

CHARLES DROVE the rest of the way, thinking hard. Everything was coming unglued. He'd known something like this might happen if anyone important ever got wind of her past doings, and apparently that was just what had happened. Half the population of San Francisco must have seen the program; his dealership would be doomed; nobody would buy a car from a man married to the murderess Barbara Eagle. What could have possessed her to submit to a television interview? He had to find a way out of this.

BARBARA RANG for her maid.

The woman appeared. "Good evening, Mrs. Grosvenor," she said. "May I get you something?"

"Pack a bag, two changes of clothes and a trench coat. I'm leaving within the hour."

"Yes, ma'am," the woman said, then fled to the master bedroom.

Barbara left her to her work, went to the bar, and poured

vodka into a glass—a lot of vodka. She knocked back half of it, then walked out onto the terrace. The sun was below the horizon, but the sky was still aglow, and the lights of the city were coming on as darkness approached.

Suddenly, she had it: they would stop in Santa Fe, and she would go out to Eagle's house and shoot him and that actress wife of his. She would do it herself this time—no middleman. Then they could continue to London, and she could begin to rebuild her life.

"South America," she said aloud. "Nobody knows me in Buenos Aires. I'll take the city by storm!"

The maid appeared on the terrace behind her. "Pardon me, Mrs. Grosvenor," she said sweetly. "Shall I pack some handbags?"

Barbara wheeled on her. "Can't you do any goddamned thing? Don't you know by now what I want and don't want?" She was spewing vodka as she screamed.

"Yes, ma'am," the maid said, then fled the terrace and went back to her packing.

CHARLES DROVE INTO the apartment building. He jumped out of the car, leaving the door open and the engine running. The doormen would take care of it. He waited impatiently for the elevator to arrive, then pressed the P button, and half a minute later the doors slid open.

He felt sick to his stomach. Now, just when he had nearly everything he wanted, she was coming apart. He knew what the flight to London would be like, and the days beyond. She could be the bitch from hell for weeks at a time, especially when she had had some upset, and this sounded like the upset to end all upsets.

He didn't want to leave San Francisco; he loved the city, and the city loved him. He had friends here, even admirers, whereas in London he was nothing but a moneyed arriviste, the creature the British upper classes despised most. He had been blackballed by the Garrick Club and White's, after he had practically forced business acquaintances to put him up for membership. He had bought a yacht, then had had to sell it at a huge loss because no top yacht club would have him, and Barbara wouldn't let him join anything less. She had made a public scene at Annabel's when they had had to wait half an hour for a table, humiliating him in front of people he wanted to be his friends, and someone from the yellow British press had witnessed the event and spread it over the gossip columns, along with his history of being blackballed. People had stopped returning his phone calls. His heart was pounding. How could he stop her from going to London? He couldn't, he realized. He was at her disposal, pure and simple.

It had to end.

The elevator doors opened, and he could see straight through the apartment to the terrace, where she stood, looking out over the city. She put a glass to her lips and threw back a drink, then set the glass on the parapet.

Charles was walking toward the terrace, then he was walking faster, then he was running. She heard him coming and glanced over her shoulder. "Where the fuck have you been?

Get me another drink," she spat, then turned back to the Bay view.

Charles went straight for her. He stopped, bent over, grabbed her by the ankles, and dumped her over the parapet. She didn't scream, she shouted obscenities all the way down, until they ended in a soft *plop*.

He didn't pause to think about what he had done; he ran back to the elevator, turned, and screamed, "BARBARA!" Then he walked quickly through the living room.

The maid appeared from the direction of the bedroom. "Mr. Grosvenor," she called at his back as he walked. "Is anything wrong?"

"Didn't you see her go over?" Charles walked to the parapet and looked down. He could hear horns blowing and brakes screeching from the street fifteen stories below. "Barbara!" he shouted.

The maid appeared at his elbow. "What's happened?"

"She went over," Charles replied, feigning shock. "As the elevator doors opened I saw her standing there, then she put down her glass and climbed over the edge." The glass stood empty on the parapet.

"Oh, my God!" the maid half whispered. "Should I call somebody?"

"Call 911," he said. "Tell them a woman has jumped from the terrace into Green Street."

The maid ran for the phone.

A feeling of relief washed over Charles. He was free of her, free at last. He could be a man again, and anywhere he wanted. He walked back into the living room, to the bar, poured himself a stiff scotch, then sat down in a living room chair. He took a swig and stared at the floor, composing himself for what lay ahead.

He was still sitting there in that pose when the police arrived.

LATER, AFTER THE eleven o'clock news, Billy Burnett, aka Teddy Fay, switched off the television and turned to Betsy. "It seems my work in San Francisco is done," he said.

AUTHOR'S NOTE

I am happy to hear from readers, but you should know that if you write to me in care of my publisher, three to six months will pass before I receive your letter, and when it finally arrives it will be one among many, and I will not be able to reply.

However, if you have access to the Internet, you may visit my website at www.stuartwoods.com, where there is a button for sending me e-mail. So far, I have been able to reply to all my e-mail, and I will continue to try to do so.

If you send me an e-mail and do not receive a reply, it is probably because you are among an alarming number of people who have entered their e-mail address incorrectly in their mail software. I have many of my replies returned as undeliverable.

Remember: e-mail, reply; snail mail, no reply.

When you e-mail, please do not send attachments, as I

never open these. They can take twenty minutes to download, and they often contain viruses.

Please do not place me on your mailing lists for funny stories, prayers, political causes, charitable fund-raising, petitions, or sentimental claptrap. I get enough of that from people I already know. Generally speaking, when I get e-mail addressed to a large number of people, I immediately delete it without reading it.

Please do not send me your ideas for a book, as I have a policy of writing only what I myself invent. If you send me story ideas, I will immediately delete them without reading them. If you have a good idea for a book, write it yourself, but I will not be able to advise you on how to get it published. Buy a copy of *Writer's Market* at any bookstore; that will tell you how.

Anyone with a request concerning events or appearances may e-mail it to me or send it to: Publicity Department, Penguin Group (USA) LLC, 375 Hudson Street, New York, NY 10014.

Those ambitious folk who wish to buy film, dramatic, or television rights to my books should contact Matthew Snyder, Creative Artists Agency, 9830 Wilshire Boulevard, Beverly Hills, CA 98212-1825.

Those who wish to make offers for rights of a literary nature should contact Anne Sibbald, Janklow & Nesbit, 445 Park Avenue, New York, NY 10022. (Note: This is not an invitation for you to send her your manuscript or to solicit her to be your agent.)

If you want to know if I will be signing books in your city, please visit my website, www.stuartwoods.com, where the tour schedule will be published a month or so in advance. If you wish me to do a book signing in your locality, ask your favorite bookseller to contact his Penguin representative or the Penguin publicity department with the request.

If you find typographical or editorial errors in my book and feel an irresistible urge to tell someone, please write to Sara Minnich at Penguin's address above. Do not e-mail your discoveries to me, as I will already have learned about them from others.

A list of my published works appears in the front of this book and on my website. All the novels are still in print in paperback and can be found at or ordered from any bookstore. If you wish to obtain hardcover copies of earlier novels or of the two nonfiction books, a good used-book store or one of the online bookstores can help you find them. Otherwise, you will have to go to a great many garage sales.